ERICA SWIFTFIELD

AN UNADJUSTEDS STORY

MARISA NOELLE

Cover art by Marisa Noelle

FIRST EDITION

The Shadow Keepers

The Unraveling of Luna Forester

The Mermaid Chronicles

Quest for Atlantis

Fight for Freedom

Ghost Pirates

Vendetta

Denizens of Darkness

Vortex Returns

The Mermaid Chronicles Companion Guide

THE UNADJUSTEDS UNIVERSE

The Unadjusteds Trilogy

The Unadjusteds

The Rise of The Altereds

The Reckoning

Prequel/Companion Novellas

Silver Melody

Matt Lawson

Joe Rucker

Erica Swiftfield

Paige Starling

Hal Small

Kyle Lewis

Jacob Shea

Sawyer Watson

Addison Shields

President Bear

For the dreamers who believe the world can be rebuilt, one act of courage at a time.

CHAPTER 1

THE THOUGHT CIRCLES Erica's brain with more aggression than a bulk crashing into a human opponent on the field. It's been on her mind all day. Through Maths with Mr. Reynolds and his malfunctioning EmotionAmp ring that makes everyone in a ten-foot radius drowsy, through recess when she nibbles on a few slices of apple, through dance practice when she falls off the top of the pyramid and bruises her button nose on the crash mats. That wouldn't have happened if she had wings.

If her mom and dad haven't reneged on their promise, that small box she eyed on the coffee table this morning is the answer to her dreams.

Erica and Jess burst through the front door, laughter trailing behind them like confetti. Arms brimming with a precarious stack of snacks, they tumble into the hallway and make a beeline for the living room.

"I still can't believe you convinced your mom to let you

open presents without her," Jess says, her warm smile whipping Erica's excitement higher.

Jess' orange wings flutter as she sets the gifts on the coffee table. Wings she's had for over a year, because her parents agreed thirteen was the right age for butterfly wings. Erica wouldn't choose orange—the garish color makes her look more sickly than beautiful—but they suit her girlfriend. Most of the time. Erica knows when to keep her mouth shut. When the right time is to tell a friend if their ass looks too big in a pair of skinny jeans or if hooking up with three guys in one night will cause the rumor mill to explode. And Jess' wings have kind of grown on her, outlined in thick, black lacing that makes the colors pop, and accented with swirling EcoTattoos. Since the transformation, Jess sticks to wearing mostly orange and black and a few other neutral tones to set the wings off. That's one thing Jess does well; fashion. And let's face it, she didn't choose the orange. It was one of the cheaper nanites, and the cheaper nanites don't come with choices. But at least she has the wings. At least *she* will make the cheer squad in high school next semester. Erica tries not to let the envy get to her. It's her fourteenth birthday after all, and if things go right, she'll be getting her own pair of wings. Purple ones.

Erica shrugs, a sly grin playing at her lips. "She knows I'm impatient. Plus, she had to fly out for that conference, so it was open them alone or—" she makes a pitiful puppy dog face "—open them with my best friend here."

Jess raises an eyebrow. "*Best friend?*"

A flush warms Erica's face. Their relationship is new. They evolved past the friend zone a couple months ago, but she hasn't told anyone yet. Her parents aren't quite as accepting as Jess'. And they might force a nanite on her. The wrong kind. The kind that might take her feelings away.

Erica leans over and places a soft kiss on Jess' lips.

"That's better," Jess says, punching her lightly on the shoulder. "But you're still spoiled."

"Maybe a little," Erica admits, plopping onto the couch and ripping into a bag of chips. She offers them to Jess, who takes a few and sits cross-legged on the floor. "But I'm grateful, you know. For everything."

"Especially for these!" Jess holds up a sparkly box, shaking it gently. "You're going to love what I got you."

"Gimme!"

Jess holds the box out of reach. Laughing, Erica clambers over her, pins her to the floor, and snatches the box from her hand, the chips spilling over the floor.

Jess giggles, that adorable high-pitched laugh that makes Erica's stomach feel warm and cozy. "Okay, you win!"

Erica leans forward as Jess opens the box just enough for Erica to see inside. Her eyes widen and she clasps her hands over her mouth. "No way! Jess, these are amazing!"

"I knew you'd like them," Jess says, lifting the earrings out of the box. They are iridescent and purple. *Purple.* Like her wings are going to be. "They're HoloGems."

Erica's mouth drops open. "No way!" She scrambles for the earrings, slides one into the hole in her ear, and immediately, tiny fluttering butterflies are projected flying around her head. "Best. Present. Ever!" She plants another kiss on Jess' lips, soaking in the warmth of her mouth, the feel of her skin tingling against hers. "Thank you, Jess."

"You're welcome." Jess stands and flutters her wings. "So, where is it? Are you going to open it?"

Erica eyes the small purple box her mom wrapped late last night. She thinks it contains a nanite. The answer to her dreams. And her popularity. And her existence. But then she remembers the kid who died last month when he took a bulk nanite. He wanted to be a football player. His body didn't take to the change. It happens sometimes.

"I will," Erica replies, twirling a strand of her long, dark hair around her finger. "But I want to ask you a question first..."

"Okay. Shoot. What's up?"

"Was it scary? The transformation? Did it hurt?"

Jess shrugs. "A little scary. But mostly exciting. It didn't hurt. Are you having doubts? Because if you don't want to, you don't have to."

"No doubts..." Erica bites her lip, her mind racing with possibilities. "It's just a big change. I have a low pain threshold. And I won't be able to wear that purple sweater anymore...no wing slits."

Jess laughs. "I know an alteration place. It will look even better than before."

Why is she hesitating? Wings are the only thing she's wanted for years. Not only so she'll be guaranteed a spot on the high school cheerleading team next year, but so she can fly away. Go wherever she wants. Somewhere private. Somewhere she and Jess can be alone and they won't have to worry about being seen.

Jess sits again, puts a hand on hers. "You know I'll support you no matter what, right?"

"I know," Erica says, softer now. "It's just a lot to think about."

Their fingers brush as Jess hands Erica another gift, and a spark of anticipation ignites in Erica's chest.

Jess stretches her arms above her head, then playfully flutters her orange wings. The iridescent sheen catches the light, making her look like a living flame. Erica can't help but stare; the wings have always fascinated her, especially since she added the swirling digital tattoos.

"Do they feel...real?" Erica asks, dropping the unopened gift, and Jess pauses mid-flutter.

Jess grins, turning to give Erica a full view of the delicate structures. "Touch them and find out."

Erica reaches out tentatively, her fingertips grazing the edge of one wing, an EcoTattoo vanishing from under her fingertips only to reappear in a different section of the wing. It's softer than she expected, like the finest silk, yet it holds a surprising amount of warmth. She snatches her hand back, as if she's stroked a live wire.

"It feels like I've always had them," Jess says, her voice filled with pride.

Erica sinks deeper into the couch, her thoughts drifting. "It's so crazy to think a little pill can do all that."

"It's not just a pill," Jess says, sitting next to Erica. "It's a whole process. You have to be ready for it, mind and body. The change isn't instant."

"How long did it take for you?"

Jess tilts her head, thinking. "About a month for the wings to fully grow in. But every day I could feel them. And I practiced in MetaMorph so I could fly as soon as the wings were strong enough."

Erica nods. She's clocked so many hours in the virtual reality setting that she's earned herself a bonus EmotionAmp ring. "And you never had second thoughts?"

Jess laces their fingers together. "Oh, tons. But I knew this was what I wanted. And it's not like I could go back once I started."

Erica shifts on the couch, projected purple butterflies roaming around her head. "That's the scary part, isn't it? Being stuck with the change. Did you see that guy with the hedgehog spikes the other day?"

Jess clamps a hand over her mouth, muffling her laugh. "And the woman with the turtle shell on her back?"

Erica shakes her head. "That's what you get in the discount aisle, I guess."

Jess cups her face, brushes a thumb over her cheek. "But you know you're getting the real deal. There's nothing to worry about. I'll be right here with you. If it's what you truly want."

Erica nods, picturing what people will say when they see her at school on Monday. The stares, the gasps, the gossip, the admiration. She craves it all. Erica holds Jess' gaze. She remembers when Jess was just another pretty girl in school, popular but not exceptional. The wings had transformed her, yes, but it was more than just a physical change. Jess had an aura now, a confidence that was unshakable.

"You don't have to take it today," Jess says. "You can wait."

Erica arches an eyebrow. "Tryouts are in a few weeks.

You think I'm going to let you be in line for head cheerleader? Nuh-uh—we share, remember?"

Jess laughs. "Oh my God. You are the most competitive person I know."

"Gotta be in it to win it." Erica picks up the sparkly box Jess gave her earlier and slides the other earring into her ear. Now it's a butterfly party, the tiny holographic creatures fluttering over her head and down her arms, their wings changing color in pleasing hues. Soon, she'll fly with them.

Jess' eyes soften. "Happy birthday, Erica."

Jess is about to kiss her when Erica's phone rings.

"Hey, Mom," she answers, her voice cautious.

Jess gives her wide eyes. Beautiful brown eyes that melt her heart.

"Erica, darling, how are you?" Her mother's voice crackles through the speaker, warm but distant. "I'm so sorry I haven't called sooner. This conference has been non-stop."

"I'm good," Erica says. "How's Boston?"

"Humid. I don't have long. Wanted to check in on your… transformation. Have you taken the pill yet? Is Sarah there with you? You know you can wait until I get home—"

"I'm good," Erica cuts her off. Sarah is her best friend, Jess is her girlfriend, Erica's mother doesn't need to know that it's Jess who is with her. "I haven't taken it yet. I'm working up to it."

"You can always wait for your dad—"

"No way." Erica rolls her eyes and Jess laughs. "He wanted me to get hawk wings, for God's sake. I mean brown? Really?"

"They *are* more powerful…" Her mom lowers her voice.

"I thought about getting a nanite for myself. I'm thinking blue wings. Maybe with my next bonus money."

Something tightens in Erica' s chest. The wings are her idea. Her mother never professed to be interested in nanites until now. This is Erica's dream. And she doesn't want to share it. Doesn't want to see her mother living out failed cheerleading dreams through a pair of wings.

"We could fly to the beach together…" her mom babbles on. Doesn't she know butterfly wings aren't made for endurance? The beach is miles away. States away.

"I've gotta go, Mom," Erica says. "More presents to open."

"Well, okay darling, happy birthday."

Erica disconnects the call. She picks up the purple box from the coffee table and slides it open. Inside is a tiny white pill. Erica puts it in her mouth and swallows it with a sip of soda.

CHAPTER 2

THE PILL SLIDES down Erica's throat like any other. She half expects some sort of lightning bolt, a jolt of energy, but all she feels is the fizz of soda.

"Oh wow, you just kinda went for it," Jess says. "But you need to take off your top, the wings will tear it."

Jess helps Erica out of her T-shirt until she sits on the couch in her bra. A blush warms her face, but she's not embarrassed for long as the anticipation ratchets up.

She watches Jess, waiting for her expression, but Jess just smiles, her fingers twining around Erica's. "How long does it take?"

"Minutes, maybe?" Jess says, though her voice sounds far away.

As she tightens her grip on Jess' hand, a rush of warmth blooms in her chest.

Then it starts.

Her skin tingles, and her back muscles pull tight. She

winces as uncomfortable sensations ripple from her spine, pressure building between her shoulder blades, expanding, stretching. There's no pain—just the strangest, electric pressure, as if her skin is coming alive on its own.

A purple glow washes over her, swirling over her skin, cascading down her limbs as the nanite takes hold. Jess' eyes widen, breathless, as if she's witnessing magic itself.

"Erica...your hair!" Jess whispers.

Erica feels it before she sees it, the weight of her hair changing, becoming heavier. She raises her hand to touch it, strands falling over her shoulders in waves of soft lavender. She catches her reflection in the mirror over the mantle, barely recognizing the girl staring back at her.

And then the wings unfurl.

They burst from her back in a cascade of iridescent color, each wing glimmering in shades of purple that shift with the slightest movement. They twitch with an eager restlessness, ready to take her anywhere.

Erica can hardly breathe. Jess reaches out, fingers grazing the edges of Erica's wings, her touch so delicate it sends a shiver racing up her spine. The color alters to a deep, bold violet, then to a dark crimson, then back to the violet.

"Erica, they're...they're beautiful," Jess says, her voice filled with awe. "But they're changing color."

Erica allows herself a triumphant smile. So many girls have butterfly wings now—you don't have a hope in hell of making it onto a cheer team if you don't—but she always knew hers would be different. Special.

Erica's wings deepen to a bold, neon pink, the color

reflecting the thrill surging in her chest. She laughs. "Guess I'm an EmotionAmp ring now."

Jess laughs too, a soft, delighted sound. "So, what's this color for?"

Erica doesn't answer, not with words. Instead, she takes a step closer, her wings glimmering a bright scarlet as her heart races. Her hand finds Jess' cheek, and she leans in, her lips brushing softly against Jess', a kiss filled with all the things they can't say out loud.

"Oh my god! You did it!"

Erica and Jess pull apart to see Sarah in the doorway.

Sarah stands there with her hands cupped over her mouth and her brown eyes widening more every second.

Erica turns and gives the wings a flutter, sensing instinctually how to make her new muscles work. The movement sends a delicious shiver racing down her spine. *Utterly glorious.*

Sarah rushes forward. "Are you okay?"

"Of course I'm okay," Erica says, pushing her wings wider, watching them as they cycle through all the colors of the rainbow.

"They're changing color," Sarah said. "When did they make a nanite that could do that?"

"I'm not sure they have," Jess replies. "We think the colors reflect Erica's emotions."

"It's a 'me' thing," Erica says.

"And your hair. Your eyes."

"My eyes?" Erica rushes to the mirror. Not only has her hair turned lavender, silver highlights sparkling under the dim light, but her eyes are now violet. She grins, turning her head one way and then the other. She can get used to this look. No one will mess with her now. And she will dominate the cheerleading squad. All her dreams...in the palm of her hand.

"Where have you been, anyway?" Erica asks. "I was about to open the rest of my presents."

Sarah drops her hands back to her sides and strolls further into the room. "Archery practice. I've got that competition next week."

Erica rests her hands on her hips. She can't believe how much lighter she feels. Not just because the wings support her, but because her dream has become reality. She is finally who she was always meant to be. A real, live fairy. "Maybe you should take a cool nanite too. Something fun to wow the guys."

Sarah frowns. The expression rankles Erica. "I want a guy to like me for who I am, not what I look like. Besides, I've taken enough nanites as it is."

Erica waves a hand. "Boring ones. Night vision, enhanced reflexes, elongated breath control...don't you want to...mix it up?"

Jess throws her a warning look, but Erica ignores it.

"No, not really," Sarah says, her voice strained. "I'm fine the way I am."

"Of course you're *fine*..." Erica emphasizes the word. "But, I don't know, if you got wings too, then the three of us would look so cool together. You could get a navy blue? That would add some nice tones—"

"Oh my God. Seriously. Enough already," Sarah huffs. "You're as bad as my parents."

Erica raises her palms. "Okay. Alright already. Just an idea. Keep your hair on. I don't want you to get left behind."

Sarah tilts her head, flicking her hair over her shoulder. "I'd say winning first place in nationals is hardly getting left behind."

"Yes, you're very good at *archery*," Erica says. "But it's not...I don't know...it's not the same as wings, is it? You could join the cheer team with us."

"I do not want to cheer for inflated egoists who think they're the Second Coming and chase a ball around a pitch all day," Sarah says, blowing her bangs out of her eyes. "It's your birthday, let's not make it about me."

"Okay." Erica rolls her eyes. She waits a beat, knowing she needs to lighten the mood. "How about glitter eyelashes?"

Sarah cracks a smile and gives Erica a playful shove. "Can't fault your persistence. If you don't make head cheerleader senior year, I'll—"

"Take a nanite?" Erica bats her eyelashes.

"Oh my God! Fine! Whatever. I'll take a nanite. I quite fancy a stardust skin graft," Sarah says. "Senior year. No sooner."

"Yes." Erica punches the air and her wings turn a triumphant red. "Stardust would look fantastic on you."

Jess nudges her. "Why don't we open more presents?"

"Yay! More pressies!" Erica claps. She looks at Sarah. "What did you get me?"

Sarah hands her a small package. Erica rips it open.

Inside is a purple sweater. One she can't wear now because of the wings.

"There's a gift receipt inside," Sarah says, wincing. "Clearly, I didn't think that through. You can exchange it for whatever you want."

Irritation prickles her skin. She's talked about wanting wings for as long as she can remember. And she's known Sarah for just as long. Why would she buy her a present like this?

"We can get it altered." Jess breaks the silence. "Just like we're going to do with your other clothes."

Erica chucks the sweater on the couch. "Or I'll buy new clothes. Thanks, though, Sarah."

Erica tears through the rest of her presents. Loves the new clothing her mom bought her that accommodates her wings. The WingCam from a group of girls at school is preloaded with filters in purple tones. See? They get it. They know her. Sometimes Erica wonders if Sarah understands her at all. But they are both competitive. Erica with cheer, Sarah with archery. They're bound to rub each other the wrong way sometimes. But Erica won't let their awkward moment spoil her birthday.

Things are better when her dad gets home. He cooks fried chicken and produces a cake from her favorite bakery. It's in the shape of a pair of purple wings. She grins up at him and wraps her arms around his neck before she blows the candles out.

"Happy birthday, sweetheart," her dad says.

Sarah and Jess begin the familiar song and Erica watches the mesmerizing flames of the candles until it's over. She doesn't know what to wish for, considering she's now got the thing she's spent the last thirteen birthdays hoping for. So she closes her eyes and imagines being head cheerleader, Jess on her arm publicly with no one batting an eyelid, and Sarah cheering her on.

✕✕✕✕✕

Monday arrives with a heatwave sweeping through the Kansas plains, but Erica barely notices. Her newly grown wings twitch with every step, adjusting to the breeze, reflecting slivers of morning light in flickers of iridescent purple. Her WingCam is clipped to her wing, recording every second of everyone's reaction as she passes them, and her new earrings carry her in a swarm of beautiful butterflies. Every glimpse she catches in passing windows and car mirrors makes her stomach somersault, excitement buzzing through her veins. Today, she is finally the girl with wings—and not just any wings, but a full, mesmerizing set that changes colors with her emotions. She can already hear the whispers, feel the stares, and she wants all of it.

Jess walks beside her, her own orange wings folded neatly against her back, and on her other side, Sarah trudges along with her hands shoved in her pockets. Sarah's dark hair is pulled back in her usual ponytail, her gaze shifting between Erica and Jess. She is clearly jealous. Erica can't help a smug smile spreading over her face. Sarah is finally realizing how cool a pair of wings are. Maybe she'll join her and Jess after all. If Sarah gets wings, all will be perfect in her world.

Jess tugs her forward, steering them all toward the main

doors of the school. "Come on. You're going to be late for the grand debut," she says with a wink.

Inside, the hallway buzzes with activity, and conversations halt as Erica steps through the doorway. A couple of kids gasp, one of them dropping his notebook. Erica bites her lip to keep from grinning too widely, though her wings betray her, flashing a bright, exhilarated yellow. The admiration in her classmates' eyes is intoxicating. It's like walking through a dream where she's the star, the kind of person others aspire to be. She angles her wings so the WingCam captures every single moment. So she can play it again and again.

"Erica! Those wings are insane!" a boy from her science class says, his eyes wide.

"Lavender hair?" another girl asks, her voice laced with envy. "I thought you were going for just wings!"

"Apparently, I'm a little extra," Erica says, her smile growing, her wings pulsing with pride. She glances at Jess, who beams back at her, clearly enjoying the show.

They reach Erica's locker where people have already formed a crowd. Several people edge closer, studying her from all angles like she's a rare specimen on display. She preens under the attention, flipping her hair over her shoulder and letting her wings fan out behind her, catching the light. People snap pictures and she knows she'll be all over socials within the hour. Maybe she can even become an influencer.

"So, what's it like?" a red-headed girl named Addison asks, staring at her wings.

"It's..." Erica pauses, searching for the right words,

wanting to sound effortlessly cool. "It's like breathing. Like they've always been a part of me."

The crowd murmurs appreciatively, and her wings pulse with striations of triumphant color. Out of the corner of her eye, she catches Sarah's expression—a tight, half-forced smile. Irritation prickles Erica's skin, but before she can say anything, Sarah leans in.

"This is what you've always wanted?" she hisses in her ear. "To be the girl everyone stares at?"

The question stings more than Erica expects and heat builds behind her eyes.

Jess must notice, because she jumps in before Erica can respond. "What an awesome day! Those cheerleaders at Wichita North aren't going to know what hit them."

Sighing, Sarah steps away. "Well...have a good day being the center of attention."

"What is her problem?" Erica says to Jess once Sarah is out of earshot.

Jess stares after her. "Maybe she's jealous."

Maybe she wants a flashy nanite after all, but doesn't know how to say it. Because she's taken so many already, some would call her a junkie. But not Erica. No way. If Sarah got something flashy and cool, she'd call her a hero.

The crowd disperses as the bell rings, and Erica notices a few lingering glances, some admiring, some jealous. She loves the mix, the way people look at her like she's a movie star. She heads to class with Jess, walking on air, her head firmly in the clouds. But there is a small thorn in her side with Sarah's name on it.

As they enter homeroom, Erica takes her usual seat by

the window, Jess sliding into the seat beside her. Sarah is already sat a row behind them, her head in her notebook. Erica watches her, a faint prick of annoyance resurfacing. *Why can't she be happy for me?*

The teacher, Mr. Bowen, enters, and Erica catches his wide-eyed glance at her wings before he composes himself. "Looks like we have a butterfly among us," he says with a bemused smile, glancing at Erica. The class chuckles, a few of them turning to stare at her again, and Erica's cheeks heat.

"Purple suits you, Erica," someone in the back calls, and she can't help but laugh.

The morning flies by in a blur of stares and whispers, Erica basking in the attention. By the time lunch rolls around, she's practically vibrating with excitement. There are so many moments recorded on her WingCam, they will keep her going for years. As they head to the cafeteria, she notices Sarah hanging back, her face set in a stiff expression.

"Sarah," Erica calls, turning back. "Are you...are you really mad about this?"

Sarah pauses, glancing at Jess, who gives her an encouraging nod. Sarah takes a deep breath. "It's not that I'm mad, Erica. It's just...it's like everyone's trying so hard to be something they're not. Like, what's wrong with being...normal?"

Erica's wings flicker an indignant green. "Maybe some of us don't want to be *normal*, Sarah. Maybe some of us want more."

Sarah's eyes harden, a rare fire sparking in them. "And what happens when everyone looks like you and Jess? What happens to people like me, who don't want to change?"

"Nothing will happen to you." Jess steps between them,

her wings folded away. "No one is going to force you to change, Sarah. Everyone can decide for themselves. It's a personal choice."

"I remember when you spent hours reading poetry, not flying in MetaMorph." Sarah looks at Erica sadly.

Erica shakes her head. "That was a long time ago. Kiddie poems about self-esteem. I grew up. Got some confidence. Made my dreams come true."

Jess swipes an arm between them, gaining their attention. "Why don't we grab lunch, yeah?"

Erica lets out a breath, tension ebbing as Jess' soothing presence wraps around her. "Fine," she mutters, following Jess to the food line.

The cafeteria is loud, voices buzzing as Erica and Jess approach. Heads turn, whispers follow, and the tension with Sarah fades into the background. Erica is the center of attention again, and she relishes every second, but wishes she could shake off Sarah and her bad mood. She doesn't need negativity today.

After they grab their trays, they settle at their usual table, Sarah still in the food line. Jess leans close, her voice low. "Look, Sarah will come around. She's just...she's competitive in her own way. I think seeing all this is making her feel like she's missing out. All those nanites she's taken and she really hasn't got much to show for it."

Erica frowns, nibbling on her sandwich. "But this isn't about her. It's about me, and she should be happy for me, right?"

Jess gives her a small, sad smile. "Yeah, but sometimes... when people are jealous, they don't always know how to say it." She rests a hand on Erica's, her thumb tracing circles over her knuckles. "Just give her time."

Sarah stares at them as she takes a seat on an opposite chair, her mouth set in a hard line, but Erica notices a flicker of something—maybe hurt, maybe longing. As she meets Sarah's gaze, a pang of guilt swells in Erica's chest.

Sarah's family doesn't have a lot of money. She probably wants another nanite, but is too proud to show it.

CHAPTER 3

The Kansas sky stretches endlessly above Erica, a wide, depthless expanse with a few feathery clouds floating high and away. Warm air ripples across the fields below, scented with summer grass and faintly earthy. It lifts her wings as she stands on the hilltop, toes grazing the edge. Her heart hammers with excitement and nerves; today is the day Jess will teach her to fly. The WingCam is clipped on firmly. No way is she going to miss recording footage of her first flight.

Erica's lavender wings flutter in small, restless motions, glistening in the sunlight. It still surprises her how right they feel, how natural, how ingrained. Over the past few weeks, they've grown stronger, no longer tentative or awkward, and now, when she stretches them, they respond without hesitation, sweeping wide and smooth. She's dreamed of this moment since they first took shape—since the first sharp tingle of change surged through her veins after she swallowed the nanite.

"Remember to trust them," Jess says beside her, her own

orange wings shimmering in the light. There's an ease in the way Jess moves, wings shifting effortlessly, and Erica mimics her friend's stance, lifting her chin, flexing her fingers. She hopes she looks that confident, that fearless.

Jess leans forward. "When you're ready, take a running start, let your wings catch the air...and let go. Like you've done in MetaMorph a thousand times." She flashes Erica an encouraging grin. "They'll carry you."

Erica takes a breath, lets it fill her with the warmth of the sun and the rush of anticipation. Behind her, she hears Sarah shuffling her feet in the grass, and it's comforting to know her friend is watching. After all their arguments about the wings—Sarah's doubts, her frustration that Erica would change herself so dramatically—they've finally found common ground. She's here now, with that tiny, approving smile on her face, and somehow, that's enough.

A soft breeze catches Erica's wings, and she feels the smallest lift beneath her, a tantalizing taste of what it'll be like to soar. She glances back at Sarah, who offers a thumbs-up, then focuses her gaze on the open sky.

Erica leans forward, the ground solid beneath her feet, the wind pulling her wings higher, and then—she leaps. For one brief second, she's weightless, balanced on the edge of the hill. And then—

She rises.

The world drops away, and she's floating, then gliding, the air rushing against her skin, her wings holding her up like they were made for this. She dips forward, laughing, her pulse thrumming as she glides over the fields, the ground a blur of green and brown beneath her. This is a million times better than MetaMorph.

"See? You've got it!" Jess calls, gliding beside her with a wide grin. "Now, try following me. We'll go slow at first."

Erica nods, too breathless to answer. She mimics Jess' movements, angling her wings left, then right, adapting to the subtle shifts in the wind. The air comes alive around her, buoying her, and as she glides in lazy circles, a new confidence blooms in her chest. She wants to go faster, to dive and spin, to test the limits of what her wings can do. For now, though, she breathes it all in: the sensation of flight, the weightlessness, the freedom. Her whole life, she was anchored to the ground, and now she's finally broken free.

"Sarah!" Erica calls, looking down. Sarah's standing on the hill, shading her eyes with one hand, grinning up at her. She gives an enthusiastic wave, and Erica waves back, a surge of warmth swelling in her chest.

"You look amazing, Erica!" Sarah calls, her voice a faint echo on the wind. Erica's wings pulse the shade of violet—a color that's come to mean joy, excitement.

"So, how does it feel?" Jess calls, angling her wings to float closer. Her voice is playful, but there's a knowing look in her eyes, as if she remembers exactly what Erica's experiencing now. "Not bad, huh?"

"Not bad?" Erica echoes, laughing. "It's...everything. It's better than I imagined." She wants to spin, to dive, to climb higher and see how high her wings can take her. She rises a little, the wind rushing under her wings, holding her up.

Jess flashes her a grin. "You're a natural, you know that? You were born to fly."

The words send a shiver of pride through Erica. She's worked hard for this, spent so many hours dreaming of this exact moment. Now that it's here, it feels surreal, like she's stepped into a different world. A world where she's more than just Erica from Kansas. She's Erica with wings, a girl who can do anything.

As they circle back toward the hill, Erica's thoughts drift forward, to next year, to high school. With her wings, she will be more than every other cheerleader. She will be a star. Her wings will set her apart, make her unforgettable. She sees herself in the gym, flipping through the air, her purple wings a blur, the crowd cheering. She will be everything she's ever dreamed of.

They loop back to where Sarah stands, and Erica slows, tilting her wings to descend, light as a feather. Her feet touch the ground, and she turns to Jess, breathless and glowing with excitement.

"Well?" Jess asks, crossing her arms with a smirk. "First flight was a success?"

"Better than success." Erica looks at Sarah, who's still smiling, even though Erica can tell she's a little bewildered by it all. The familiar competitive spark is in Sarah's eyes, and Erica can almost see the gears turning in her friend's mind, weighing her curiosity against her judgment.

Sarah clears her throat. "I'll admit...that was pretty cool to watch. Don't forget us little people when you're rich and famous."

Erica throws her arms around her. "You'll always be my best friend. Nothing can change that."

Jess nudges her. "Unless she goes on a date with Joe."

Erica steps back, laughing. "Yeah, no pretty boy is going to steal you away from me."

Sarah tilts her head. "You have Jess. We can double date."

Erica smiles. "Maybe." Never. She's still not ready to come out. Only Sarah knows about her and Jess, and she plans to keep it that way. As much as she adores nanites and the improvements they make, there are others that could destroy her world.

Erica looks at her feet as she recalls several stories she's heard. Being part of the LGBTQ+ community has always been problematic where she's from, but in recent years, when DNA can be altered and parents can choose for their kids to be straight...she doesn't have the words for it, only simmering anger that could explode into rage. Nanites are a choice. Optional. For improvement. Not for...not to support homophobic campaigns.

She reaches for Jess' hand, then takes Sarah's too, clenches her teeth against the heat of forming tears. She is Erica Swiftfield. She is exactly who she wants to be, and no one will change that.

The three of them stand there, looking out over the fields, the warm Kansas sun dipping lower in the sky, casting their shadows long and far. And now Erica has the sky to escape to too, if she ever needs it.

CHAPTER 4

Erica is wingless and grounded, standing nervously outside the gym. Her heart gallops in her chest as she imagines what's about to come: the jeers from more experienced girls, the hard landings, the sheer humiliation of appearing like a try-hard. She glances at Jess, who's staring at the closed gym doors with the same nervous expression.

Jess reaches for her hand, gives it a tight squeeze. "We've got this."

Erica pushes the doors open. The gym is a riot of color, sound, and nervous energy as fifty girls mill about, stretching and practicing routines. She takes a deep breath, imagines it filling her with the same cocky assurance as the girls inside, and steps through the double doors.

The noise level ratchets up: a cacophony of shrieks, laughs, and the occasional thud of someone hitting the mat. Jess shrinks back, but Erica tugs her forward, right into the thick of it. A tall girl with blue streaks in her hair and an even bluer set of wings brushes past them, not-so-subtly knocking Jess to the side.

"Hey!" Erica starts, but Jess just shrugs.

"It's...whatever. Come on, let's find a spot."

Erica is tiny compared to the older girls, a mere wisp of a freshman, but her confidence is unshakable. She knows she has what it takes.

They carve out a tiny patch of space and start their stretches. Erica's eyes flick around the gym, taking in the various cliques and tandems. Almost every girl has wings—small, decorative things that don't even look functional. Butterfly wings, dragonfly wings, swan wings, and even a pair of holographic wings. All courtesy of nanites.

"Can you believe this?" Jess whispers, bouncing on her heels. "It's like a butterfly farm in here."

"We'll fit right in," Erica says, holding her chin high.

"Totally," Jess agrees, giving her a quick knuckle knock.

A tiny pang of envy pricks her as she watches a girl with ladybug spots flutter up to retrieve a water bottle from the top of the bleachers. She never thought about polka dots. But, she reasons, she's the only person in existence whose wings change color.

"The football team is here too." Jess juts her chin at the guys hanging out on the opposite bleachers.

Erica's gaze snags on a muscly freshman. He's still unadjusted. He hasn't taken a bulk nanite. But there's still time for that. Half the team is still unadjusted. For now.

Erica turns her attention back to the present. On how much rides on these tryouts. On how different things will be if she makes it. If they both make it.

A whistle pierces the din and all heads turn to a toned woman in her early thirties. She's wearing a tank top emblazoned with a stylized eagle, the school's mascot. Her left shoulder sports a half-sleeve tattoo; a set of wings. But she looks unadjusted.

"I'm Coach Henderson," the woman announces. "We're so pleased you all came. We've got a ton of talent this year, so the competition's gonna be fierce." She pauses, letting the words sink in. "We're looking for more than just skills. We want girls who are dedicated, who have spirit. Who can bring it *every single game*."

Erica swallows. A rush of confidence flashes over her skin. She has spirit and skills in spades. Both she and Jess do. She steals a look at Jess, who pumps her arm in a signal of solidarity. Erica can't help but smile.

The coach runs through the agenda: warm-ups, individual skills, then a short routine. Erica's mind races. She's practiced every move a thousand times in her room, in the backyard, even in the aisles of the grocery store. She knows she can do this. She has to.

The warm-ups pass in a blur of stretching and jogging. Then come the individual skills. One by one, girls step forward to show their jumps, tumbles, and stunts. Erica watches intently, sizing up the competition. When it's her turn, she takes a deep breath and steps into the circle.

Her body moves on autopilot: a high kick, a cartwheel, a perfect toe-touch jump. She lands softly, like a cat, and hears a few murmurs of approval. The coach makes a note on her tablet. Erica's heart soars.

The last part is the hardest: a short routine performed in

groups. Coach reads off names and the girls scatter to different parts of the gym. When she gets to Erica's group, Erica almost sighs with relief: Jess is in the same one. They make their way to a corner where eight other girls are already huddling. Erica recognizes a few of them: Claire Thompson, a junior with a reputation for being ruthless; Eliza Park, sophomore class president and perpetual overachiever; and the blue-haired, blue-winged girl who shoulder-checked Jess earlier.

"Hi, I'm Taylor," says the blue girl. "Just so you know, I'm already on the team, so this is more like a practice for me."

"Of course it is," Claire says, rolling her eyes. "Let's get this over with."

Someone produces a tablet with the routine loaded on it. Erica cranes her neck to see and immediately feels dizzy; the moves are fast and intricate, a blend of acrobatics and dance. The kind of thing that takes weeks to perfect, not twenty rushed minutes, but it's not the hardest routine Erica's performed. It's a mash-up of everything they've already shown off, set to a peppy cheer track. They get one run-through before the music starts.

Erica nails every move, her body in perfect sync with the music and her teammates. She even catches Jess' wobbly handstand, saving her from a faceplant. When the routine ends, Erica is breathless and exhilarated. She looks at the coach, who gives a curt nod, a wisp of a smile. Maybe she's not so severe after all.

The girls retreat to the bleachers for a break. Erica can hardly sit still. She eavesdrops on the seniors sitting behind them who are scoring the tryouts.

"I got agility last week. I can jump so much higher."

"I went for speed. My wings are a blur of pink now."

"I got added strength. After the last time I ripped a wing…"

"I got all three. There's a discount going on at Adjusted Athletics."

The seniors have taken multiple nanites. Erica hasn't thought about more. Thought the wings would be enough, but clearly she needs to up her game.

She looks at Jess, who widens her eyes, then shrugs. "I can't afford any more."

Erica has been saving for months for a BioMusic account, but maybe her money would be better spent elsewhere. She wonders how much they are, if the discount is still taking place.

"You were amazing, by the way," Jess says.

"So were you."

Jess shakes her head. "I almost ate the floor."

"But you didn't. We killed it." Erica believes it. She has to believe it. They're going to make it. Together.

After another two grueling hours of practice, Coach Henderson blows her whistle. "That'll do. I want to congratulate all of you on your effort. This was one of the toughest tryouts we've had. Remember, the list gets posted tomorrow. Now go get some rest."

Erica and Jess exchange a hopeful glance. They exit the gym, and the evening air cools their sweat-dampened skin.

"We did our best," says Jess. "No matter what happens, we gave it our all."

Erica laughs. "There's no way we haven't made the cut."

"Okay, but, you know, a little humility?"

Erica scans the parking lot. Wings, tails, scales, extra fingers...if you can think it, it exists. There's no room for humility in their world. Not anymore. You have to take what you want. Or grow it.

They walk with their arms linked to where Jess' family's driverless car waits in the lot. As they approach the car, Jess pulls Erica into a hug.

"We've got this," Jess whispers.

The public hug surprises Erica, but she leans into it, taking comfort in Jess' arms.

"See you tomorrow," Erica says, as Jess hops into the car.

Erica waves as the car slides away. She stands alone in the parking lot, savoring the last bit of summer twilight. No matter what, tomorrow everything will change.

She begins the walk home, her mind replaying the day's events. Each step is a countdown to the future she's always dreamed of. She watches the footage her WingCam recorded and cringes at Jess' handstand. So unlike her. And it looks bad. Doubts creep in. She doesn't sleep. Or maybe she does a little. Her dreams are filled with feathers and wings and flips and she wakes with a tight coil of nerves in her stomach. She tells herself for the millionth time there is nothing to be nervous about.

After watching the sun rise, Erica slips out of bed and makes her way to school. She makes a beeline for the gym. A small crowd has gathered around the bulletin board, and she recognizes a few of the girls from tryouts.

"Do you see it?" one girl exclaims, and another squeals.

Erica's stomach performs a few flips. She edges closer,

standing on her tiptoes to peer over the shoulders of the growing mass. The list is typed in neat columns, with a header that reads "Varsity Cheer Squad."

She scans the names, her eyes moving with the frantic pace of a hummingbird. Halfway down the list, she sees it: Swiftfield, Erica. A tidal wave of relief crashes over her, followed by a dizzying high. She made it. She actually made it.

Of course she did.

But then she notices another name. Monroe, Jess. It's at the very bottom, with an asterisk next to it.

Her mind races. What does the asterisk mean? Her thoughts are interrupted by the sound of Jess' voice.

"Did you check it yet?"

Erica turns to see Jess running down the hall, a huge, hopeful smile on her face. She freezes, not knowing what to say.

Jess slows as she gets closer, breathing hard from her sprint. "Well?"

Erica bites her lip. "I made it."

Jess' face lights up. "That's awesome, Erica! I'm so happy for you!" She rushes to the list, and Erica watches as Jess' eyes zero in on her name. The pause is excruciating.

Jess turns back, her expression unreadable. "I'm an alternate."

Erica's heart sinks. "I'm sure you'll still get to—"

"Yeah," Jess interrupts, forcing a smile. "It's better than nothing, right?"

The hall grows silent as the other girls disperse. Some

celebrate, but most walk away with slumped shoulders. Erica stands rooted, guilt gnawing at her insides.

"Don't worry," Jess says. "I'll still come to all the practices and stuff. It'll be just like we imagined."

"Jess, I'm really sorry. I wanted this for both of us."

"Don't be," Jess says, her voice turning brittle. "This is great. You're in. I'm happy for you."

Erica wants to say more, to make Jess understand how much her support means, how she wouldn't even be here without her. But the words tangle in her throat.

"We should get to class," Jess says, walking away slowly.

Erica follows, her feet dragging. The day stretches ahead of them like an endless road, and for the first time, she wishes she could skip to the end.

They walk out of the gym and into the main corridor. The school is a maze of cinder block walls and linoleum floors, still sparkling from the summer break's deep clean. Lockers clang as students make their morning rounds, and the air buzzes with the static of a thousand simultaneous conversations.

Erica taps Jess on the shoulder. "Hey, you got your car here? Can I get a ride to—"

"Yeah, sure," Jess says, not letting Erica finish. "But it has to pick up my mom at five."

They stop at Erica's locker, and she fumbles the combination, taking four tries to tap it in correctly. She swears under her breath. Jess waits, her hands in the pockets of her jeans, rocking on her heels.

Erica opens the locker and from inside, her phone beeps. She catches the sound of several other phones receiving alerts. She glances at the screen. It's an advertisement for the Adjusted Athletics store, with a big, bold headline that reads, "Back to School Sale! 50% Off All Nanites!"

She shows it to Jess. "Do you think they're really that cheap now?"

Jess shrugs. "Some of them. Why?"

"I was thinking...if I had extra agility or speed, I could be top of the pyramid. It could help the team."

Jess raises an eyebrow. "I don't know...that's kind of heading into junkie territory."

"Is it?" Erica sighs. "It's just...practical. We need every advantage we can get. Maybe if you'd had one you wouldn't be an alternate. That's how Sarah has achieved so much with her archery, how many is it now—"

"The nanites Sarah has taken are really minor."

"I know, but—"

"Don't start pressuring her into something flashy again. I think she's reached her limit."

Erica laughs. "There's no limit on nanites. Didn't you see that documentary on NanoReel—?"

"The one about Jacob Shea who's started teleporting in his sleep?" Jess replies with a dubious expression.

"Pah!" Erica waves her hand. "Teleportation is class ten. I'm not suggesting Sarah get something like that, but wouldn't it be cool if she had wings? Like us? Or, I don't know, a funky tail to keep her balanced..."

"Didn't you hear about that kid over the summer who overdosed? Took five nanites and died?"

Erica rolls her eyes. "That's because they were all class ten. All physical. I'd never be that stupid...but I need something to put me over the edge. Didn't you hear all the seniors talking about how many they've taken?"

Jess shoves a hand through her unraveling ponytail. Her hair has blue tips today. "Yeah, but leave Sarah out of it."

"She's *my* best friend—" Erica snaps.

"I'm just saying," Jess interrupts, swiping the advert away. "Don't do anything drastic. You're perfect as you are. And so is Sarah."

"It was just a thought."

The first-period bell rings, and the hallway surges with students heading to class. Erica and Jess stand in the middle of the stream, momentarily islanded together.

"I'll see you in biology," Jess says, and before Erica can respond, she's gone, swept away by the crowd.

The rest of the day is a blur for Erica. She goes through the motions of her classes, but her mind is elsewhere—on the list, on Jess, on the glittering wings of her fellow teammates. When she's not lost in the butterfly storm produced by her HoloGem earrings, she wonders if her parents would let her take another nanite. But if it's not a physical change, they don't need to know.

By the time she gets to biology, her last class of the day, she's exhausted from the repetitive cycle of thoughts. She slides into her seat next to Jess, who is already dissecting the syllabus with the zeal of a mad scientist.

"We're lab partners again," Jess announces, and Erica can't tell if she's happy about it or merely stating a fact.

"That's great," Erica says, trying to muster some enthusiasm. She flips through her own syllabus, not paying attention to the words on the page. The teacher drones on about safety procedures and the importance of wearing goggles.

Halfway through the class, Jess leans over and whispers, "I'm sorry."

Erica's head snaps up. "For what?"

"For being a bitch this morning," Jess says, her eyes downcast. "I'm happy for you, Erica. I mean it."

Erica's chest tightens. "You're not a bitch, Jess. You have every right to be upset."

Jess shakes her head. "I want you to know I support you. No matter what."

Erica doesn't know what to say. *Thank you* feels inadequate, and *I'm sorry* feels patronizing.

She puts a hand on Jess', and they sit in a warm, understanding silence for the rest of the class.

When the final bell rings, Jess turns to Erica. "Do you want to come over? We can practice a few routines."

Erica hesitates. She's tired, and she wants to lie down and let the day dissolve. But she owes Jess. Really, it's the least she can do.

"Sure," she says. "Let me text my mom and tell her I don't need the car to pick me up." Erica shares a self-driving car with her parents. She's been urging them to get a second for ages, because their schedules keep clashing, and now that Erica will be traveling all over the country for cheer competitions—hopefully, definitely, absolutely!—they're going to need two cars. Which is why she often gets a ride with Jess, who only has to share with her mom.

They walk to the parking lot, and Erica sends a quick message to her mom, letting her know where she'll be.

"I had an idea," Erica says. "About the asterisk."

Jess looks at her, hopeful.

"Maybe it means they're giving you a week to, like, prove yourself. You know, as a trial run."

Jess purses her lips and tilts her head. "That would make sense. Henderson said this was one of the toughest tryouts. Maybe she couldn't decide. And I wasn't the only one with the asterisk by my name."

Erica nods, glad that Jess' optimism is returning. "You'll crush it. And then we'll be set."

The girls get into the car. The ride to Jess' is filled with small talk—nothing important, but enough to smooth out the rough edges of the day. With the press of a button, Jess tints the windows, then leans in close to Erica. They share a brief kiss while no one is watching, but the usual sparks are missing. Erica deepens the kiss, searching for their connection, pressing herself against Jess, her folded wings flicking between purple and blue. Finally, the stress of the day melts away. In the car, just the two of them, they are Erica and Jess again.

When they pull into Jess' driveway, a strange mix of dread and hope engulfs Erica. One kiss isn't going to solve everything.

Jess' house is a small, two-story cottage with a chipped blue exterior and an overgrown garden in the front yard. Inside, it's cluttered but cozy, filled with the kind of knick-knacks and memorabilia that Erica's mother would have trashed during one of her quarterly purging sprees.

They head to the backyard, which is a tangled mess of

grass and dandelions. A rickety wooden fence surrounds the perimeter, giving it the feel of a sunken pirate ship.

Jess stretches her arms and does a quick cartwheel. "Okay, let's start with the eagle set."

They fall into formation, and Erica watches as Jess moves with the fluidity of water, her motions second nature. Erica matches her rhythm. After a few runs, their sync is perfect, their movements creating an invisible thread of unity.

"How's it feel?" Jess asks.

"Good," says Erica, though she's not sure if she means the routine or something else entirely.

They practice for an hour, running through different sets and talking strategy. Jess offers tips and suggestions, and Erica listens, absorbing every word. By the end, they're both sweaty and tired, and the tension between them is a distant memory.

"That helped get rid of my stress," Jess says, lying on the grass. She looks at the sky, which has turned orange with the setting sun, matching Jess' wings.

Erica sits next to her, hugging her knees. "I'm glad you're feeling better."

Jess closes her eyes.

Erica studies the lines of her face, the way her cheeks have a perpetual rosy hue. She remembers the first time she saw her. That golden brown hair flying wild during flips at the drill team tryouts—she had green tips then. That bold, unflinching confidence had won Erica over in an instant.

"I should go," Erica says, not sure why she's suddenly in a rush to leave.

Jess opens her eyes and sits up. "Yeah. Don't want to wear you out before our big debut."

They walk to the front yard. Erica's house is only a few blocks away, a short walk. She turns to Jess and hesitates, searching for the right thing to say.

"Thanks for...everything," she says.

Jess waves it off. "It's nothing."

But it's not nothing. It's everything. They've spent so many hours training together. Jess introduced her to a myriad of important video clips and famous cheerleaders to help improve her technique. Without that knowledge and all the practice hours...Erica would be the alternate.

"I'll see you tomorrow," Erica says, starting to walk away.

"Erica," Jess calls.

Erica turns back, wishing she could touch her, kiss her.

They share a meaningful look, and that is all that is needed to communicate what they're feeling.

Before she turns the corner, she turns and waves to Jess, who stands in the driveway until Erica continues walking. When she gets home, she goes straight to her room and collapses on her bed. She lies there, staring at her phone, re-reading the advertisement for the Adjusted Athletics store, wondering if she could stop by before school tomorrow.

CHAPTER 5

THE NEXT DAY dawns with an oppressive humidity that makes the air feel like wet cotton. Erica dresses slowly, deliberately, as if rushing might tear the fragile fabric of her wings. She's both excited and terrified for the first practice. She's a freshman and she made the varsity team. She must stay on the ball. The next few days will define her reputation for the duration of high school.

When she arrives at school, she heads straight to the gym. The halls are empty, save for a few early-rising teachers and staff. She likes the quiet, the way it makes the school feel like a set after the actors have gone home. She can be whoever she wants to be.

In the gym, the cheer squad is gathering. There isn't a single person in the room who doesn't possess a pair of wings. Not all of them are butterflies. There are bird wings too, as well as a small collection of other insect wings. She was right to insist on a nanite for her birthday, or she wouldn't be standing here now.

The older girls stretch their wings while they chat. A pang of envy hits Erica—for how well they know each other. There is an obvious hierarchy, the head cheerleader commanding all the attention. That could be her. That *will* be her.

"Erica!" someone calls, and she turns to see Jess walking toward her, holding a tray of smoothies. "I got us breakfast." She hands one to Erica. "I got everyone breakfast."

Erica laughs as she accepts the cup. The cold seeps through the paper and into her hands, a brief reprieve from the morning's heat. "You're such a suck up."

Jess cracks a grin. "It's a proven method."

The girls swarm around Jess as she hands out smoothies, calling their thanks, and patting her shoulder.

"Looks like it's working," Erica says.

Jess winks as she takes a long slurp.

Coach Henderson walks into the gym, blowing her whistle. The sound puts a stop to the chatter, and the girls gather around her. Erica and Jess make their way to the circle.

"Congratulations to all of you for making the team," Coach Henderson says. "And a special welcome to our new members." She pauses, and Erica's chest tightens with anticipation. "We have a lot of work to do before the first game, but I have no doubt this will be a strong squad."

Pride surges through Erica. This is real. She's part of something bigger now. She is on the way to realizing her dream, and she's only fourteen years old. This is the result of dedication and ambition.

Coach Henderson continues, "I know some of you have questions about the list. Jess," she says, looking directly at

Jess. "Heather, Rosie and Mercedes, your spots as alternates means you'll be called up if anyone can't perform. You'll practice with the team and be ready to step in at any moment. And that happens more than you'd think. We can only approve regeneration nanites for juniors and above. Our tricks are dangerous, and we do incur injuries."

Erica glances at Jess, who nods stoically.

Coach Henderson divides them into groups, the alternates with one of the senior cheerleaders who will take them through the routine. Erica is placed in a group with the head cheerleader and she can't stop the grin stretching across her face.

Coach claps. "Now, let's get to work."

The team divides. Jess walks off. There is a tug in Erica's chest, like a string being pulled too tight. This isn't how it was supposed to work out, but Jess being an alternate is out of her control. And as Coach said, she may well get plenty of airtime. Erica turns to her group and throws herself into the drills, all of them using WingCams to record their progress.

Coach Henderson runs them through conditioning exercises, basic routines, and partner stunts. Erica's body aches, but it's a satisfying pain—the sort that comes from pushing limits.

Jess and the other alternates participate in all the drills, working just as hard as the rest of the team. During a water break, Erica chats to Jess.

"You're doing great," she says.

Jess wipes her forehead with the back of her hand. "Thanks. It's easier when you don't have the pressure."

Erica frowns. "What do you mean?"

"I'm just practicing. You guys are the ones who have to perform."

Erica doesn't like the way Jess is distancing herself, as if she's already written off her chances. She wants to hold her hand, to hug her, to kiss her. But they can't do any of that here. "You could be called up anytime."

Jess laughs. "You make it sound like the army."

"Less bulk, more flutter." Erica flaps her wings, the delicate material fanning Jess' flushed face. "We're in this together, you know."

Jess searches Erica's face. "Yeah. I know."

The rest of the practice goes by in a sweaty blur. When it's finally over, Coach Henderson blows her whistle and calls the team together.

"Good work today," she says. "Don't forget to stretch. I'll see you all Thursday."

Cheerleading is going to fill all Erica's time with twice-a-week practices, games on Friday nights, and the private coaching her parents agreed to—she won't risk becoming an alternate, or worse, being dropped. She hopes Jess won't make too many new friends without her. That she'll understand. That resentment won't come between them. Because if their roles were reversed, Erica wouldn't be able to look at Jess without seeing green.

Feeling a flush of guilt, she scans the gym for Jess, but she's already heading to the locker room.

"Jess," Erica calls. Jess turns, and Erica jogs over to her. "Do you want to come with Sarah and me to the diner?"

Jess frowns. "I thought you were starting your private cheer lessons today—"

"Next week," Erica says.

Jess smiles. "Actually, that would be nice."

After they change out of their uniforms, they fall into a comfortable silence as they walk to the diner. Despite the heat, Erica reaches for Jess' hand and they lace their fingers together. That small touch is enough to calm the anxiety that's been circling Erica's stomach since her wings grew. But maybe it's not anxiety. Maybe it's anticipation. Excitement. Exhilaration. Knowing that her future is currently being defined. Everything is going to be okay.

The diner is a small, family-run operation that's been in the neighborhood for decades, standing strong amid the myriad of fast-food joints that have popped up all over the place with extra windows for bulks and winged adjusteds to place their orders. The air conditioning hits them like a wall of arctic wind as they enter, and Erica savors the goosebumps sprouting on her skin.

Sarah is at a table when they arrive, three slushies sitting on the surface. "I got one of each flavor. Thought we could share."

Erica smiles as they slide into the booth.

"Thanks," Jess says, sitting next to Erica, their thighs pressed close.

"It's been ages since we did this," Sarah says. "I hope we can do it more often."

"Your archery schedule is pretty brutal," Jess says. "And now Erica's got extra cheer practice..."

Erica taps the table. "We'll make time. It's important."

Jess looks at Erica. "Yeah," she says. "It is."

"How did practice go?" Sarah plants her chin in her hand.

Erica and Jess share a look.

"It was intense," Jess says.

"Coach thinks we can make nationals again this year," Erica adds, thinking of the Adjusted Athletics advert she saved on her phone. The agility nanites ones are only a few hundred dollars. She almost has enough.

"Those national teams have taken so many nanites." Sarah rolls her eyes. "It's a wonder they still look human."

Erica bristles. "So have you!"

Sarah gives her a sly grin. "Yeah, but you can't tell, can you?"

"What's that got to do with anything?" Erica demands.

"The nanites I take are super minor. Small changes. They leave me unadjusted."

Erica frowns. "That's how you see yourself? As an unadjusted?"

"I guess." Sarah shrugs. "There's a difference between physical and mental changes."

"Is there?" Erica asks, genuinely curious as to how Sarah sees this divide.

"I guess it's not about whether someone is unadjusted or adjusted," Jess says, stirring her slushie with a straw. "But *how* adjusted they are."

"Different professions require different enhancements," Erica says, her irritation acting like a stubborn extra layer of skin.

"Exactly," Sarah says. "Taking invisible nanites means I

can play it to my advantage. My opponents often underestimate me because they don't know if I'm adjusted or not."

Jess laughs. "Don't you have to declare what you've taken?"

"Only in the nationals," Sarah says. "Trying to level the playing field when there are so many combinations of nanites is pointless, so they don't bother enforcing restrictions."

"I guess it becomes a competition of poor versus rich," Jess mutters.

An uncomfortable silence falls between them. Money is a sore spot for Jess. Erica went with her to buy her nanite and she had to choose the cheapest one in the shop. Orange. Weaker fabric. Shorter wingspan. Money really does buy happiness. If Jess had more money, she could have bought better wings, and then maybe she'd be on the squad and not hanging on as an alternate. Erica's family isn't rich by any means, but she made damn sure her parents understood the importance of the nanite class system, that they couldn't buy her a random pair of wings from the bargain basement bucket. That was one reason she had to wait until she was fourteen, so her parents could put enough money aside.

Jess takes a slurp of her slushy, her cheeks hollowing and the drink squelching as she sucks.

To take the focus off Jess, Erica turns to Sarah as she winds a finger into her lavender hair. "I reckon you should go for it. Take something outrageous. Something so flashy that it distracts your competition. If you turned up with something funky...a vibrant tail...or I don't know, why not wings? You'd look so cool. Social media would make you the poster child for archery."

Jess squeezes her thigh, which Erica interprets as a message to back off, but Erica has never backed off from anything, and she was doing this to take the focus off Jess, so she shouldn't be complaining.

Sarah rolls her eyes. "I'm not interested in social media or being a poster child. I just want to nock arrows."

"I hate seeing the way people look at you at school." Erica takes a sip of her drink and curses the fact that her wings are turning acid green. They only glow that color when she's angry or lying.

"Excuse me?" Sarah narrows her eyes. "How do people look at me?"

Erica stalls. Those words kind of popped out. She didn't mean to hurt Sarah's feelings. But high school has only recently started and it's not quite turning out how she imagined it. So many kids get nanites over the summer break between middle school and high school and now the halls are a myriad of showy wings and tails and kids racing with superspeed or teleporting into the girls' changing rooms, and such. There are only a few tables in the cafeteria where the unadjusteds sit, and even though Sarah has probably taken more nanites than anyone, she looks unadjusted, she sits with the unadjusteds, and she acts like an unadjusted. If she would just take a damn pill, a proper one...then they could spend more time together.

"That came out wrong," Erica admits. "But...things are changing. You either have to jump on the train, or, I don't know, drown trying? I don't think I said that right either." She sighs. "I miss you. I miss you sitting at our lunch table—"

"I don't eat with you guys anymore because I'm sick of

scratches and cuts on my face from all the wings at your table."

"I'm sure that's it," Erica says.

Sarah shakes her head sadly. "You said you wouldn't change when you got your wings."

"Maybe it's not me who's changed," Erica bites back.

Jess leans over the table to sever their conversation. "Are you guys going to Joe's party this weekend?"

Erica's heart gives an extra beat and her wings shimmer in an infatuated lilac. Joe Rucker. Plays football, but he's not a bulk. Just an unadjusted. Although she is with Jess, she's not immune to the good looks of the guys. But he's off limits. He's got his eye on Sarah, apparently. And Sarah has her eye on him. So they can have at it and be in an unadjusted-looking bubble together. Whatever. At least she has Jess.

"I'm going," Sarah says. "But I'll be late as I have a competition in Kansas City."

"Can't," Erica says. "My brother is home for the weekend."

"I'm going with Heather and Mercedes," Jess says.

Erica raises a brow. "The other alternates?"

Jess shrinks. "Yeah. Thought we'd bond over our loser status."

Sarah flicks Jess' shoulder. "You are not a loser. If I was Coach, I'd pick you as my head cheerleader."

Jess laughs.

"Thanks a lot," Erica mutters.

Sarah raises her hands. "It's not always about you, Erica."

"I never said it was."

"Then stop acting like it is," Sarah snaps.

"Jeez, have you got your period, or something? There are nanites for that, you know."

Sarah lurches to her feet. "It's been a couple weeks since we hung out. I gave you space because I know how important cheer is to you. But clearly this was a mistake."

Erica stands to face her. "That's not fair. You're busy with archery too."

"Maybe I am." Sarah crosses her arms. "But I don't cut down my friends."

"I'm sorry if that's how you feel."

"But you're not sorry."

"I just said I was sorry."

"No, you didn't."

"Guys!" Jess waves her arms in the air. "Can we calm down, please? You guys have been best friends since you were born. You don't need to fight." She sighs. "Maybe this is my fault. Maybe I got in the way."

Sarah shakes her head. "This is not about you."

"For once, I agree with her," Erica says to Jess, lightly touching her arm.

"You guys clearly need to talk. Calmly, and get to the bottom of whatever's eating you," Jess says.

Sarah raises her gaze to meet Erica's. "It would be nice if you came to a competition. You haven't been to one since I started two years ago."

"It would be nice if you'd been more supportive of my wings," Erica said.

"I came with you on your first flight."

"But you don't approve."

"That's not true. I don't care what you do, wings just aren't right for me."

Jess rubs her forehead. "So it seems you both disagree on nanites."

Erica shrugs.

"Yes," Sarah replies. "I guess so."

Erica stares at her best friend. "Aren't you tempted to get something fun?"

Sarah sighs. "Sometimes. It might be nice to fly away for a while, get away from the pressure...but I don't want to be like every other fairy...no offense."

"I'll try not to take that personally," Erica says, swallowing her irritation in an attempt to keep the peace. "But times are changing. If you don't embrace the flashier nanites, you'll be labeled an unadjusted. And I have a feeling it's not going to end with separate lunch tables."

Sarah sighs.

"I'll never stop being your friend," Erica says. "But I don't want to see people picking on you and treating you like shit. A nanite is an easy way out of that. I was thinking of going to Adjusted Athletics Saturday morning. They're having a half-price sale. Thought I might get an agility nanite. You could come with me. See what there is. See if anything appeals. It doesn't have to be big. Maybe cute little horns on your head."

Sarah gnaws on her lower lip. "Maybe."

Jess smiles at them. "See? That wasn't so bad."

A few minutes later, they are all hugging goodbye on the sidewalk before they walk home in their different directions. Erica stands on the street, the asphalt radiating heat like a summer grill, watching as Sarah's figure disappears from view. It's about time she came around. Things would be so much easier for her if she joined her as a true adjusted. Maybe she's finally starting to see sense. And then they can stop fighting and get back to how they used to be.

Erica walks home, her mind whirring with possibilities, wondering which nanites will be available at Adjusted Athletics. Now she just needs to get her parents on board.

When she gets home, her mom is in the kitchen, chopping vegetables. "How was practice?"

"Good," Erica says. "Tough, but good."

"Can you set the table? Dinner will be ready soon."

Erica goes to the dining room and removes the ceramic plates her mom favors from the sideboard. She sets them down carefully, then places utensils next to them with practiced motions.

Her mind drifts back to the advert. She knows if she's going to compete at this level, the wings aren't enough.

She walks to the kitchen, where her mom is sautéing something in a pan. "Mom," she says. "Can I ask you something?"

Her mom turns, wiping her hands on a dishtowel. "What's up?"

Erica hesitates. "I'm thinking about taking another nanite. All the seniors have taken four or five...and if I want to stay on the team, I'm going to have to level up..."

Her mom frowns. "How can they all afford that?"

Erica shrugs, her wings turning a nervous yellow. This will be so much easier if her mom gets on board. "Some of them get sponsored. Scholarship deals at school. Parents. Or they saved up, like me."

Her mom comes closer, and Erica shows her the advert on her phone. "I thought you said wings were all you needed," her mom says.

"I did," Erica says quickly. "But things change. I didn't realize how competitive the squad was. We could go to nationals...and win! And the nanites are on sale."

Her mom studies the advert, and Erica tries to read her face. Her mom has strong opinions about this kind of thing, but she's always been willing to listen.

"Your father and I worked hard to give you every opportunity," her mom says slowly. "We've never wanted to buy success for you."

"I'm not asking you to buy it." Erica bristles. "I've worked damn hard to get where I am—"

"I know you have, sweetheart. It's just...it's a slippery slope..."

"I'm only doing what everyone else already has."

"I don't know, Erica."

"I have to level the playing field, or I won't make it." Erica hated the pleading tone in her voice. "I can use my own money."

Her mom hands her phone back. "I think you need to decide what's most important to you: the appearance of success, or the real thing."

Erica looks at the advert, the 50% off sign a magnet to her ambition. "So you wouldn't be angry?"

"I'd be disappointed," her mom says. "But it's your life, Erica. You need to make your own choices."

Erica nods, absorbing her mom's words. She didn't say no. She flutters her wings, marveling at the depth of color. There is no question what she will do. She is not a junkie. She won't be like that senior Priscilla who's taken over ten nanites, but she is determined to stay on top.

She'll do whatever it takes.

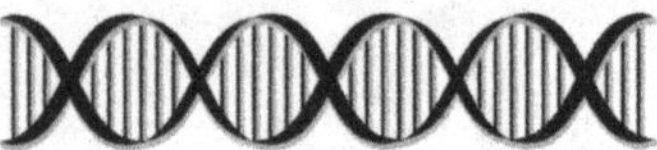

CHAPTER 6

WEEKS BLUR into a kaleidoscope of practices, games, and social events. Erica throws herself into cheerleading with the ferocity of a tiger on NanoBoost, thanks to her two new nanites; agility and flexibility. She learns every routine, every chant, every tradition, and wonders if she should opt for a voice projection nanite next. It might save herself from a case of laryngitis.

The older girls, once intimidating, become her mentors and friends. They take her under their shimmering wings, and Erica basks in the glow of their acceptance. Her social media presence grows. Thanks to her WingCam and regular posting, she has over ten thousand followers on EvolveMe. And when she logs on to SynchWorld to practice daring flight simulations, her virtual room floods with others who want to watch her. And the comments. Not a single troll among them.

The senior girls, once aloof and unapproachable, start to acknowledge her. It's little things at first: a nod in the hallway, a quick "nice job" after practice. She realizes they're paying attention, that they see something in her. They invite her to parties. It's intoxicating, this new life of hers, and they insist on watching replays of her daring acrobatics. The recognition sparks a flame inside her, one that grows hotter with each passing day.

"Can you believe it?" she says to Jess one afternoon after practice. "Rachel Summers just friended me."

"Who is that?" Sarah asks.

"On EvolveMe? No way!" Jess says, her face lighting up and her EcoTattoos swirling with excitement.

"She's the head cheerleader," Erica replies.

Sarah peers at Erica's phone. "She has like fifty thousand friends. It's not exactly exclusive."

Erica shrugs. "Still, it's something."

Later that afternoon, Erica and Jess are changing after practice in the locker room, a sacred space filled with the smell of sweat and the chatter of girls. Erica likes to linger here, soaking in the atmosphere. Today, she notices Jess hurrying.

"Got to bounce," Jess says, pulling a hoodie over her head. "Mom's organized one of her family bonding sessions."

"Wait," Erica says. "Are we still on for Saturday?"

Jess pauses. "For what?"

Erica's heart sinks. "The sleepover. To watch the state competition and make signs for the pep rally."

"Oh," Jess says. "I thought...yeah, sure."

"You thought what?"

Jess bites her lip. "I thought you'd be going to Sarah's birthday thing."

Erica had completely forgotten. Sarah had only sent her the invite on Monday.

"It's not the same night," Erica says. "I can do both."

"Okay. Great. Just don't wear yourself out with the extra cheer too, yeah?" Jess says, and Erica doesn't like the tone. It's not the usual Jess, not the bubbly, supportive girlfriend. It's something harder, more brittle. "I'll see you Saturday."

Before Erica can respond, Jess is out the door.

Erica sits back, letting the wooden bench dig into her spine. She remembers the promise she made to Sarah: wings or no wings, they'll still be besties. But promises are tricky things, she realizes. They don't always bend to fit new circumstances. The thought troubles her enough to keep her away from socials and spend her time listening to BioTunes in the hope the mood-altering music will chase away her negative thoughts. But her heart weighs a little heavy when she arrives at Sarah's house the next day. It's been weeks since she's been over. Sarah has been so busy with her archery.

The small, two-story home oozes with personality and vibrant color, books and sports equipment strewn about. Sarah's mom calls her Fairyca and gives her a big hug, showering Erica with warm, maternal love, but the affection only serves to highlight how long it's been since she's visited.

The birthday party is low key. A dozen friends from the archery team, a stack of pizzas, and a homemade cake. Erica feels out of place in her cheerleader's jacket, like a bulk at a beauty pageant.

She stands in the corner of the living room as Sarah opens a mountain of gifts. She looks around for Jess, who was in the kitchen making punch, hoping to soak in some comfort from her presence.

"Erica!" Sarah yells, holding up a new pair of sneakers. "Aren't these awesome?"

Erica forces a smile. "Totally."

She's happy for Sarah—really, she is—but her mind is elsewhere. It's on the gift she brought, the one she's not sure she should give her.

Sarah's mom brings out a cake, its top a jungle of candles and sprinkles. The whole room bursts into an off-key rendition of "Happy Birthday," and Sarah beams with unfiltered joy.

The song finishes, and Sarah takes a deep breath, filling her lungs to capacity. She closes her eyes, makes a wish, and blows. The candles splutter, their smoke curling upwards like tiny spirits. The room erupts in applause, and Erica claps along.

"Come get some cake!" Sarah's mom announces. The crowd shifts toward the kitchen, leaving Erica and Sarah alone.

"I saved the best for last," Erica says, walking over to Sarah and offering a small, beautifully wrapped box.

Sarah smiles. "I don't think a book of poems fits in that box."

"I didn't..." For the last five years, Erica has bought Sarah a book of poems. A love they both share. Or used to. Erica hasn't looked at a poetry book for months, and she completely forgot about the tradition. "This is better."

Sarah's eyes widen. "Erica, you didn't have to—"

"Just open it," Erica says, her tone more urgent than she intended.

Sarah takes the box and unravels the ribbon, then peels back the paper. When she sees what's inside, her mouth forms a small, silent "oh." It's a pill, clear with a sparkly core, like a piece of crystallized confetti.

"It's a lucky dip," Erica says. "You don't know what you'll get until you take it. Could be wings, could be cat eyes, could be something totally random."

Sarah closes the box. "Erica, I don't—"

"I thought you'd be excited," Erica says, her voice tight. "This is a big deal. Do you know how much these cost?" Erica delayed her own purchase of the voice projection nanite for this.

Sarah looks at Erica, her expression conflicted. "Why would you spend that much?"

"Because it's what I thought you wanted but were too afraid to say...I want you to have the same chance I did. To evolve. To fit in."

Sarah opens her mouth to speak, but no words come out. She glances toward the kitchen, then back at Erica.

"Look," Erica says, softening. "You don't have to take it right away. It's just...things are changing so quickly now, and I want you to have something that can help. Didn't you hear the president on the news last week? It's the future."

"I don't know," Sarah says. "My mom—"

"It's your decision."

Sarah bites her lip, holding the box like it's a live grenade. "Erica..."

Before Sarah can finish, Jess approaches, a wary look on her face.

"What's going on?" Jess asks.

"Erica gave me a nanite," Sarah says. "It's a lucky dip."

Jess' eyes flash with something—anger, disbelief, Erica can't tell. "Sarah, you don't have to—"

"It's a gift," Erica says, cutting Jess off. "She can do whatever she wants with it."

The three girls stand in a triangular standoff, the sounds of the party distant and muffled. Erica waits for Jess to explode, to say something that will tear them apart, but Jess holds her tongue.

"Come get your cake, Sarah," Mrs. Lin says, appearing in the doorway with a platter. Her gaze sweeps between them, taking in the tension. "You girls okay?"

"Fine, Mom," Sarah says, walking toward the kitchen. She stops and looks back at Erica and Jess. "Thanks, Erica. Really."

With Sarah out of earshot, Erica turns to Jess. "What?" she says, defensive.

Jess shakes her head. "I just...I don't get why you're pushing her so hard. She's not you, Erica."

"I'm not me either," Erica says.

Jess raises an eyebrow. "What does that mean?"

Erica winds a finger into her lavender hair. Her wings cycle through a few different colors, which makes Jess frown. "It means I'm trying to figure out who I am, and it's not as easy as staying the same forever."

Jess' eyes narrow. "You think I'm staying the same?"

Erica shakes her head. "No. I think you're figuring it out

too. But you're...always so sure about things. Nothing phases you."

Jess snorts. "That's not true."

"Your mom supports our relationship," Erica says. "Mine would send me to a conversion camp. Or buy the nanite."

Sympathy flickers in Jess' eyes. "That's different."

"Is it?" Erica gathers her thoughts. "All I've ever wanted was to be head cheerleader. For you to be right there by my side. For Sarah to support us. For her to do well with archery. But it all seems to be slipping away...because of—"

"Nanites," Jess whispers. "They're dividing the country."

They stand there, two figures in the over-heated living room. "I don't want to lose you."

Jess' orange wings flutter as she touches Erica's hand. "You won't."

Sarah joins them, her eyes blazing, the pillbox in her hand. "I think I want to do this."

Erica grins.

"You don't have to," Jess says. "We love you just the way you are, don't we Erica?"

"Of course," Erica says. "But I'm so excited for you!" This will make everything better. The awkward tension. Her relationship with Jess. They can all sit at the same table in the cafeteria again.

"I do have a question though," Sarah says.

"Ask away," Erica says.

"Will I still be me?"

Jess smiles.

Erica laughs. "Of course. I haven't changed, have I?"

Sarah breaks into a grin. "Well, I'd say you're arrogance has notched up a few levels."

"That's my school personality. You know I'm as cuddly as a kitten around you guys."

"Yeah, a kitten with claws," Jess laughs.

Erica waggles her eyebrows. "You know you love it when I scratch your wings."

"How do you two...without crumpling your wings...never mind, I don't really want to know" Sarah says.

And in that moment, it feels like it always used to. The three of them, carefree and happy. Not a care in the world. No tension between them. This is how it will be again.

"Even the president has enhancements," Erica says, wings flashing an insistent crimson. "He's got grizzly bear and black widow DNA. How badass is that? It's the future, Sarah."

Jess chimes in. "The president is a fascist meat puppet. Who cares what he does?"

Erica's wings flare red again. "At least he's doing something. He's pushing us forward."

Sarah bites her lip. In her hand, the small sparkly nanite pill glistens like forbidden treasure. "It's permanent, right?"

Erica leans in. "It's a lucky dip. They only go up to class level three, so it won't be anything major. Probably not anything as flamboyant as wings." She gives her a reassuring smile. "I made sure to enter your personal details for the best match."

"Maybe Sara's taken enough already." Jess' hair is a riot of orange, to match her wings, and she's wearing a denim jacket with patches that scream things like "PRO-CHOICE" and "VARIETY FOR THE WIN."

"Can you ever have enough?" Erica counters. "This is the future, Sarah. If you don't make it in the archery world...what are you going to do?"

Sarah's shoulders slump as a lone, deflated balloon drifts across the ceiling like a tired moth. "I'm so tired of the pressure. I'm tired of being normal. I'm tired of...I don't even know what I'm tired of."

Erica holds her hand. "I'm here for you."

"We're both here for you," Jess adds.

Sarah examines the nanite, her brown eyes wide and curious. "This could be really fun."

Sarah's archery friends have mostly filtered out, parents beckoning from doorways. Only a core group remains: Erica, Sarah, Jess, and a couple others who linger in the periphery, hesitant to leave the scene of such a momentous occasion.

"Are you sure lucky dips are safe?" Sarah's voice pulls Erica back. She sounds more skeptical than scared, which Erica takes as a good sign.

"Parents buy them at school fairs all the time," Erica says, waving a hand dismissively.

Sarah looks around the room, at the stack of presents, the half-eaten cake, the faces of friends who now look more like spectators. She bites her lip.

"There's no pressure to take it now," says Jess. "You can save up and buy what you really want after you've researched it."

Erica holds back a growl in her throat. Why can't Jess leave things alone? Sarah is about to take the pill. It's what they all want. It will make thing so much easier.

"Fine," Sarah says, and a collective breath is drawn from the room. "I'll do it."

Erica's wings flare a triumphant sunflower yellow as Sarah holds the pill to the light. The nanite glistens like liquid diamond, full of promise. She hopes Sarah can see the beauty in it, the potential for transformation.

"Happy birthday," Erica says, wishing someone had bought her a lucky dip when it was her birthday.

Erica holds her breath as Sarah chucks the pill into her mouth. She hesitates, then swallows, and the pill is gone.

For a moment, nothing happens. The room is a study in anticipation: wide eyes, tensed shoulders, hushed whispers. Then, slowly, Sarah's expression shifts. A half-smile forms as she loosens her stance.

"I don't feel any diff—" she starts, but her words are cut off by a sharp intake of breath. Her hands fly to her throat, and her eyes go wide with terror.

"Sarah!" Erica cries, but she's rooted to the spot, unable to process what she's seeing. This isn't how it's supposed to go. It's supposed to be quick, painless, like flipping a switch.

Sarah staggers, knocking over a stack of gift boxes. The room explodes into activity: kids shouting, chairs scraping against the floor, one of the lingering parents rushing forward only to get tangled in a bunch of balloons.

Erica's mind races. She remembers hearing about rare allergic reactions. They're supposed to be one-in-a-million. She guesses Sarah's is that one.

"Someone do something!" a girl shrieks, and Erica snaps into motion. She lunges for Sarah just as her friend collapses, body hitting the floor with a sickening thud.

"Call 911!" Jess yells, already pulling out her phone. She drags a kid who's paralyzed with fear toward the door, then barks at him to find an adult.

Erica cradles Sarah's head, her hands trembling. "You're gonna be okay," she lies, her voice small and breaking. "It's just shock or something. You're gonna be fine."

Sarah's lips are blue. Her chest heaves in futile, drowning breaths. Erica's wings droop, their usual brilliant colors washed out and pale. She flicks her WingCam off.

Sarah's parents rush into the room, knocking Erica out of the way as they huddle around their daughter on the floor.

The first tear streaks down Jess' cheek as she runs back, phone still in hand. "They're on their way," she says, her voice cracking with the strain of held-back sobs. She looks at Erica, then at Sarah, then away, as if the sight is too much to bear.

Time stretches and warps. Every second is a punch to the gut, each one landing with the dull thud of impending doom. She thinks about all the times Sarah has been there for her: the late-night study sessions, the first time she tried to fly, the quiet moments of being together. She can't lose her. Not like this.

"Stay with us, Sarah," Erica pleads, but Sarah's eyes are glassy, unfocused. The sound of footsteps in the hallway makes Erica look up, hoping for a miracle, but it's only the remaining kids heading outside to give them space. They shuffle out like a funeral procession.

Sarah's mom cries. Her dad performs CPR.

"Erica," Jess says softly, but Erica can't look at her. She knows what she'll see: the blame, the accusation, the righteous fury of someone who needs a target for their grief. She can't take that from Jess. Not from her.

The room is empty now except for the five of them. Erica, Jess, and the limp, altered form of Sarah Lin being cradled by her parents.

"Erica," Jess says again, more forcefully this time. "We need to—"

But whatever Jess thinks they need to do is lost as the wail of sirens cut through the evening air. Erica's heart seizes, and for a moment she foolishly believes that the sound alone can shock Sarah back to life, that the promise of help will breathe hope into her friend's lungs.

CHAPTER 7

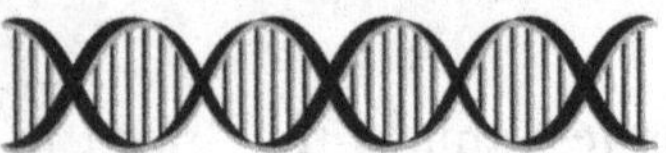

THE AMBULANCE BAY IS CHAOS, a collage of urgent motion and static worry. Erica stands alone, her wings as dull as asphalt and heavier than a bulk's dumbbell, watching through sliding glass doors as paramedics swarm Sarah's gurney. One barks orders into a walkie-talkie, another pumps a manual ventilator with desperate, rhythmic squeezes. Sarah disappears inside.

They sit in plastic chairs for hours. Erica and Jess and Jess' mom. Not talking. Just sitting and drinking revolting cups of machine coffee that scald her hands through the thin plastic.

"It's time we went home," Jess' mom says. "I start work in a couple hours. We'll call in the morning for an update."

Jess nods, then stands and stretches.

Jess taps Erica's shoulder, a gesture so light she barely feels it. "Are you coming?"

Erica shakes her head. She doesn't need sleep. Couldn't. Not with Sarah in the bowels of the hospital fighting for her life. She looks at Jess, remembers how during the drive here, Jess had refused to look at her, how she stared out the passenger window in stony silence.

"I'll wait," Erica says, her voice hollow. She can't leave.

"Will you be okay on your own?" Jess' mom asks.

Erica gives her a slight nod. Jess stares at her, a frown forming, her mouth pursing to say something, but she remains quiet.

"Come on, Jess," says Jess' mom, but Jess doesn't move. She uncrosses her arms, takes a step toward Erica, then stops.

Erica's breath catches, waiting for the reprieve, the understanding, the forgiveness.

"We'll send the car back for you," Jess says, and Erica's heart sinks. Even if they do, it won't matter. Her mom has put the car at her disposal.

The two walk away, leaving Erica with the sound of rushed footsteps and beeping machinery. She sinks into a plastic chair, its turquoise color mocking her with its cheerfulness. Her mind drifts to the empty nanite box, to Sarah's hand opening with a fatalistic flourish. She sees herself in that moment, wings blazing, urging Sarah on.

She buries her face in her hands, hoping to squeeze away the memories. A door whooshes open, and she looks up, hopeful, only to see a doctor in scrubs walking toward a waiting family. He says something, and the mother collapses in relieved sobs. The father hugs his two children, ruffling their hair with gratitude.

Erica stands and walks to the reception desk. A tired-looking nurse eyes her warily.

"Is she...?" Erica starts, but her courage fizzles. She doesn't know what she'll do with the answer.

The nurse sighs. "The girl from the birthday party? She's stabilized, but it was touch and go. You should thank the first responders."

Relief washes over Erica, followed soon after by a crushing wave of guilt. She almost wishes the nurse had scolded her, said something to unload the weight in her own chest. The anger of others is easier to bear than compassion.

"Can I see her?" Erica asks, even though the idea fills her with dread.

"Family only," the nurse says, then turns back to her computer, dismissing Erica with the clatter of a keyboard.

Erica walks back to the sliding glass doors and peers outside. The night is cool, and her breath mists on the glass. She traces a finger along the glass, making a half-hearted swirl, and watches as the condensation erases her work. She thinks about the archery set she bought for Sarah for her tenth birthday, along with the poetry book. Plastic arrows with suckers on the end. So long ago now. She wishes she could turn back time. Maybe Jess was right. Maybe nanites should never have been created. The thoughts cycle through her head. No amount of BioTunes or scrolling through EvolveMe shifts her mood.

She goes straight from the hospital to school. No sleep. Not even the projected butterflies from her HoloGem earrings can mask the circles under her eyes. Whispers follow her through the halls, morphing into accusations when she's out of earshot but not out of range. She catches snippets: "I heard she forced Sarah…" and "They were fighting, and then…" and "Sarah's in a coma because…"

At lunch, she sits alone. The entire cheer squad skips past her table, and she remembers how just last week they all piled into her booth at the diner, laughing and making obscene gestures with French fries. Now they're a pack of hyenas, waiting to strip her flesh.

The worst is Jess. She sits with the squad, talking and eating, but Erica notices how she doesn't laugh, how she doesn't once look in Erica's direction.

Three days pass like this. Each one longer and more punishing than the last. Erica starts to dread waking up, to fear the routine of getting dressed and going to school. Friday nights used to be the highlight of her week, cheering all the football players. But now she stands in the background, afraid to shout too loud, afraid the color of her wings will give her away.

On the fourth day, she gets the news. Sarah hasn't made it. She died in the night.

Erica stares at the message from Sarah's mom. Even though the words are written in black and white, she doesn't believe them. It can't be true. Not Sarah. National archery player. All those trophies she has in a glass cabinet. All that potential. She can't be gone. It can't be true.

Erica crumples in half, can barely suck in air as her lungs give out. Maybe she should get a nanite to increase her lung capacity. It would help with the cheers. She barks out a bitter laugh at the thought.

She walks home, taking the long way through winding residential streets. She thinks about the friendships she's built and the ones she's let crumble. About the person she's become and the person she wants to be.

When she gets home, she goes straight to her room and collapses on her bed. Her wings splayed behind her, a kaleidoscope of conflicted colors. She stares at the ceiling, letting her thoughts swirl and eddy like a flooding river.

Her phone buzzes. She ignores it at first, too drained to deal with whatever new drama the world wants to throw at her. But it buzzes again, then again, and she reaches for it with a defeated sigh.

It's Jess. Three messages. The first reads, "We need to talk." The second, "I'm sorry." The third, "I still love you."

Erica closes her eyes, a tear squeezing out from the corner of one. She's not sure she's ready to face Jess. Everything is so tangled, so knotted up with the events of the past week.

She opens her eyes and types, "Meet me at the park," then hits send.

Erica sits up and walks to her closet. She opens the door and looks at herself in the full-length mirror on the inside panel. Her wings are a mess of colors, an emotional slideshow. She tries to imagine herself without them, as the girl she once was: plain, unadjusted, a creature of the ground.

Could she go back? Would she, if given the chance? The wings have brought her so much—beauty, popularity, a sense of belonging—but they've also cost her. She thinks about the switch, about the gamble, and about who she'd be if she didn't take that pill.

She shrugs into her denim jacket. The one Jess helped her alter to allow for her wings, and heads out the door to the park. Jess stands by a towering oak tree, her wings drooped in a contrite slump.

"Hi," Jess says, no hint of a smile.

Erica steps into the shadow of the tree. "Hi."

They stand in awkward silence, the kind that used to be filled with comfortable knowing. Erica studies Jess' face, the way her eyes flicker with hope and fear. She remembers the first time they kissed, how Jess pulled her in with such confidence. That memory is from a different lifetime.

"I'm sorry," Jess starts, but Erica holds up a hand.

The late afternoon sun casts long shadows, and a light breeze carries the scent of blooming lilacs. The sounds of the neighborhood fill the void. Children shout and laugh, a dog barks, a lawnmower drones in the distance. Erica's wings rustle, a background whisper to her tangled thoughts.

"Erica, please. I need to—"

"I know," Erica says, turning to face her. "But I need to say something first."

Jess bites her lip and nods.

"I pushed her because I thought it would be easier for her than it was for me. She'd already taken so many nanites. What was one more? I hated seeing the way people were treating her because she looked unadjusted." But that wasn't it. Erica had spent the last few months surrounded by the most popular seniors. She didn't want Sarah to drag her rep down. That was the crux of it. "I thought if she took something physical, everything would go back to the way it's always been. We'd be on equal footing and she wouldn't resent me for changing. For leaving her behind."

"Erica—"

"No, let me finish." Erica takes a deep breath. "I never imagined it would go wrong like that. I wanted her to be loved, like I have been loved. I wanted everyone to see her true potential. To see her for who she really is. Which sounds crazy, I know. To take a nanite to become something you're not only for people to see the real you..." she trails off, unsure of her argument, unsure of how she feels. She doesn't know who she is anymore. "I never wanted her to die."

"Of course you didn't."

Erica looks away, toward the playground where a group of kids take turns on a slide. "I'm scared, Jess."

Jess gnaws on her lower lip. "You can't take it back."

"I know."

"So much has happened."

"I know that too."

"Everything has changed."

Erica hangs her head. She knows it's not just Sarah's life ending that Jess is talking about. "Is it too late? For us?"

Jess expels a gentle breath. "I think I need to be on my own for a while."

Erica swallows around the tension in her throat. "Because of what I did."

Jess shakes her head, then nods, flutters her wings. "I need time to think. The nanite issue is complicated. We both have wings. Sarah took a bunch of class-two nanites. But you pressured her to take more and I don't know how I feel about that—"

"I didn't want her to die—"

"I know. I know that. But I need a minute. With President Bear endorsing an official government nanite program...I need to think. Cheerleading is one thing. War is entirely another."

"War?"

"That's where this is all heading."

Erica blanches. War? The idea is preposterous.

"Haven't you noticed?" Jess asks. "How unhappy people are? How many unadjusteds don't come to school anymore? How pressured Sarah felt taking more and more nanites?"

"I..." In truth, she hasn't noticed. She's been too busy practicing her cheer routines and hanging out with the seniors. There are no words to absolve her of her actions.

The two stand in a heavy silence, the kind that compresses time and space.

"I fell in love with you as you were, Erica. Not as you are now."

Erica's heart breaks, not because Jess doesn't love her adjusted self, but because she finally understands. The switch, the gamble, the mask. All of it. She changed. Of course she did. It was inevitable.

"I don't miss her," Erica says softly. "The old me." That is the stark truth. Does it make her callous? Selfish? Arrogant? But her life improved when she took that nanite. And she'd do it again.

"That makes me really...sad." Jess toes the ground and a tear runds down her cheek.

They let the silence take them, each lost in their own memories of the girl Erica used to be. The sun dips lower, and the breeze grows cooler, less inviting.

"What happens now?" Erica says. She wishes she could

see the future, would know what path to take to make every-thing right.

"I don't know," Jess says. "But I think we need to figure out who we are now. Separate from each other."

Erica folds her wings away. Right now, they feel like a dirty little secret. "Yeah. I guess you're right."

Jess steps closer and kisses Erica on the cheek, a bitter-sweet gesture that carries the weight of their entire relation-ship. "Take care of yourself," she says, then turns and walks away.

Erica watches her go, not moving, not calling out. When Jess is out of sight, Erica sits on a bench by the pond. Ducks glide on the water, their lives so simple and unadjusted. She thinks about the person she used to be, the person she is now, and the person she wants to become.

She doesn't know if she can make it all balance, but for the first time in a long time, she's willing to try.

CHAPTER 8

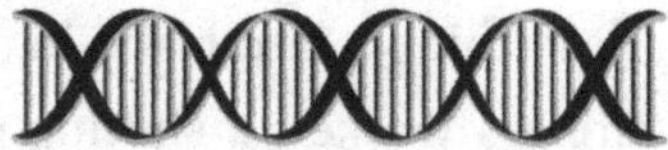

THE SKY IS a dreary wash of gray, like an old photograph faded by too many years. Erica stands at the edge of the small crowd, her wings dull and listless, absorbing the muted sorrow of Sarah's parents, of the archery team, of every person who has a reason to miss her. She feels smaller than she ever has, like a child playing dress-up in her mother's oversized emotional responsibilities.

A sob breaks the silence, raw and jagged, like glass scraping over stone. Erica winces, her attention snapping to the source: Sarah's younger sister, Mai, who is clinging to their mother with desperate hands. The sight pierces Erica, and she looks away, unable to bear the Lin family's grief piled on top of her own.

Bright clusters of flowers speckle the cemetery grounds, a riot of color against the eternal green of the shrubbery. Erica's wings shift restlessly, the colors fluttering between blue and violet before settling back into a defeated gray. She knows she should say something to Sarah's parents, offer them comfort, but there are no words to take their pain away. *I'm sorry* doesn't even begin to cover it.

She scans the crowd again, hoping to see Jess' familiar face. They haven't spoken or messaged once in the last ten days.

The eulogy starts, and the crowd hushes. Words float over Erica's head, describing a Sarah she hardly recognizes: a fearless friend, a tireless worker, a shining example. It's not that the words are untrue, but they're so one-dimensional, like reading the outline of a story without any of the rich, messy details that make it real. Erica remembers the first time she dragged Sarah to a dance practice, the look of utter horror on her face when the squad attempted a human pyramid. She remembers the hours they spent in Sarah's room, Erica prattling on about boys and lip gloss while Sarah dutifully worked through her archery physics theory. Even then, Sarah was the smarter of the two, the more focused. The sensible one.

A pang of guilt strikes her as she recalls the last conversation they had before her party. It wasn't even a conversation, really. More of an argument, and a stupid one at that. She had accused Sarah of being unsupportive, of not understanding what it was like to balance so many things at once. As if Sarah didn't have her own load to carry. As if Sarah hadn't supported her in everything...until the wings.

Erica's eyes flit to the closed casket. She knows what's inside: Sarah's favorite archery jacket, the one embroidered with a dozen different competition patches.

No one knows what the nanite was. Her body fought the transformation, and they gave her anti-transformation drugs in the hospital. But she still died. Because of a lucky dip. There is an investigation taking place into the batch number. They are supposed to be the safest pills in the country. But not for Sarah.

The thought makes Erica's stomach turn. She pushed Sarah so hard, not just in that last fight, but throughout their entire friendship. Pushed her to conform, to fit in, to change. She believed—no, convinced herself—that she was helping Sarah. That once Sarah took the leap and enhanced herself properly, with something that would boost her social status, she would be happier, more accepted. Would Sarah have taken that nanite if Erica hadn't insisted? And there lies the rub. Erica wonders if stubbornness was the real source of Sarah's strength, the thing that kept her grounded when everything else was shifting like sand, the thing that told her she was perfect how she was. And she was perfect. Without the nanite. Because she was true to herself. Erica can see that now.

The voice giving the eulogy cracks, and Erica tunes back in long enough to catch the words "tragic accident" and "taken too soon." She bites her lip, hard enough to hurt, as the memory of that day comes rushing back: the balloons, the cake, the small perfectly wrapped box.

They said it was a reaction because she'd already taken fifteen nanites. *Fifteen.* Erica had no idea it was that many. It might have happened on the next one her parents gave her anyway. But Erica's guilt won't desert her with that excuse. No. This is her fault.

The eulogy ends, and the crowd disperses, forming smaller, more intimate circles. Erica stays rooted to her spot, afraid that if she moves, she'll shatter. She watches as Mai places an arrow on the casket, her tiny hands trembling. The scene blurs, and Erica realizes she's crying, though it feels like someone else's tears.

She turns to see Jess, her tall frame and orange wings a contrast against the more traditionally dressed mourners. Erica feels a flicker of relief, but it dies quickly when she takes in the look on Jess' face: not the tenderness she's been yearning for, but something hard and unyielding.

The realization that she will never have the chance to make things right sinks in, and she feels utterly alone in her grief.

Jess says nothing. She just stands there, arms crossed, eyes fixed on a point somewhere over Erica's shoulder. The silence is a living thing, growing and stretching between them, filling the space with its oppressive weight. Erica wipes her cheeks with the back of her hand, sniffling softly. She wants to ask Jess why she's late, but she won't disrespect Jess' wishes by intruding on the space she asked for.

The service shifts into a lower gear, the kind of slow-motion grief fest where time stretches and bends. Erica's heart thumps with a painful irregularity, like a butterfly trying to break free from being pinned to a corkboard. The guilt gnaws at her, a voracious parasite feeding on her insides. This is all her fault. She doesn't need any reminders.

"Erica," Jess says at last, but it's not a start to a sentence. It's a whole statement in itself, a summation of everything she's been holding back. Erica's throat tightens, and she braces for whatever comes next.

"You should go talk to her parents," Jess continues. "They're alone up there."

Erica glances toward the casket, where Mr. and Mrs. Lin stand hand in hand, a fragile duo in the center of a dissolving human circle. Jess is right, but the idea of confronting their sorrow makes her knees turn to water.

"I will," Erica says, though she's not sure if she means it. "In a minute."

Jess uncrosses her arms, and for a brief, flickering instant, it appears she's going to take her hand. But Jess lets her arms fall to her sides, sighs, and turns away. "Whatever. You do you."

Erica watches her go, her wings sagging with the rest of her. She doesn't move to stop Jess, doesn't call out or plead. What would be the point? Instead, she stands there, a hollowed, sunken version of herself, and tries to summon the courage to do what she knows she must.

Gradually, her feet obey her will, and she makes her way toward the Lins. Each step is an effort, like walking through a field of molasses. She rehearses what she's going to say in her head: *Sarah was the best friend I ever had. I can't believe she's gone. If there's anything you need...*But even in her mind, the words sound wooden and insincere, like lines from a badly written play.

She's almost within speaking distance when Mrs. Lin looks up and sees her. There's no anger in her eyes, no accusation. Just a deep, all-consuming sadness that makes Erica want to crumble. How can they be so composed? What would her parents be like if it was her in that cold, wooden box?

"Erica," Mr. Lin says, his voice a tired whisper. "Thank you for coming."

"I—I wouldn't miss it," Erica stammers. "Sarah meant so much to me." The lie hurts. It's not that Sarah didn't mean a lot to her; it's that she now realizes how much more Sarah should have meant. How much more she could have meant if Erica had been a better friend.

Mrs. Lin releases her husband's hand and takes a step toward Erica. For a terrifying second, it seems like she's going to pull Erica into a hug, and she's not sure she could withstand that kind of tenderness. But Mrs. Lin stops short, her hands clasped together as if in prayer.

"We know she forgave you," Mrs. Lin says.

Erica's breath catches and her heart sinks. Do they blame her too? They should.

"She told me you had been arguing," Mrs. Lin continues. "The two of you always worked things out in the past. We're sure she didn't hold any grudges."

Erica feels like she's been punched in the gut. Worked things out. Had they really? In her mind, she sees the tally of conflicts and resolutions, and realizes that most of them were her getting her own way, with Sarah quietly conceding. She had thought them equals, but now she sees the imbalance, the skewed friendship where one person gave and the other took.

"It's my fault," Erica croaks out the admission.

Mrs. Lin shakes her head, places a hand on Erica's cheek. "It's not your fault. Please don't blame yourself. We'd already planned to give her another nanite that night. We thought they were safe..." tears form in her eyes and she is unable to continue.

"We're the ones who gave her the first fifteen," Mr. Lin says, his voice gruff with emotion. "It's our fault."

It seems they all played a role in causing the death of someone they deeply cared about.

"She loved you, Erica," says Mrs. Lin. "Remember that."

"I—" Erica starts, but the words choke her. *I loved her too*, she wants to say, but now she's not sure if that was ever true. Can you love someone and take them for granted at the same time? Can you love someone and consistently put your own desires ahead of theirs?

The Lins wait for her to finish, to say something that will explain her silence. But Erica has nothing. She swallows, nods, and turns away, walking back to the crowd.

The funeral ends, but for Erica, the real challenge has just begun: facing the guilt that threatens to consume her.

CHAPTER 9

"TAKE ANYTHING YOU WANT," Sarah's mother says, her voice warm but distracted. Erica notices the deepening worry lines on her face, lines that weren't there six months ago.

"We would love her things to go to someone who will appreciate them," Sarah's mom continues. "Someone who knew her."

Erica's throat flexes with a dry swallow. *Knew.* The past tense punches her in the gut.

"Thanks, Mrs. Lin," she mumbles. "I'll take a look around."

Sarah's father appears in the hallway, holding the youngest Lin daughter on his hip. The little girl is all fidgets and squirms, a bundle of unspent energy. "Dinner's almost ready," he says. "You're welcome to stay, Erica."

Erica hesitates. The Lins have always treated her like family, even when Sarah was practising her archery and unable to hang out with Erica. But being here, in this house full of memories, is almost too much.

"Maybe next time," she says, trying to sound grateful and not like she's about to burst into tears. "I just want to—"

"We understand," Sarah's mom says, cutting her off but not unkindly. "Take your time."

Erica trudges up the stairs to Sarah's room. The door is shut. She stands there, staring at the marked paint work, afraid to open it. Afraid of the flood of memories that will wash over her. Afraid that it will feel like a tomb.

Steeling herself, she pushes the door open. The room is exactly as she remembers it: the bed covered with a bedspread decorated in green and gold leaves. Archery medals hang from the bedpost, a haphazard tangle of ribbons and metal. The walls are covered in DigiFrames that portray images of famous archers and a few nature scenes in a constant scroll. A small desk is buried under a landslide of books and papers.

Erica steps inside and closes the door behind her. The room feels alive, like Sarah could walk in any moment and tell her to get out because she's trying to study. That thought almost makes Erica smile.

She walks over to the bed and sits down, running her fingers over the fabric. How many times has she barged in here, talking a mile a minute about the latest school drama or dragging Sarah to some ill-fated social event? Too many to count. And now she would give anything to have just one more occasion to interrupt.

Her eyes wander to the desk. Among the clutter, she spots a photo in a cheap plastic frame. It's of the two of them, taken three summers ago at the state fair. They're in front of the archery booth, and Sarah is holding a giant stuffed panda, grinning like an idiot. Erica looks less thrilled, rubbing her sore fingers from her disastrous attempt to draw a bow.

Erica picks up the photo and traces Sarah's face with her finger. She was so sure taking the butterfly nanite was the right thing, that it would propel her to a level where she could help her friends. Where she could help Sarah. But instead, it created a gulf between them, a rift that widened with each new enhancement, each new responsibility.

"I'm so sorry," she whispers to the empty room.

She sets the photo back on the desk and lies on the bed, wings stretching to their full extent. The nanite changed more than her DNA; it altered her perception of the world, made her see everything in terms of opportunity and advantage. How could she have been so blind?

The sound of a young squeal drifts up from the kitchen. It cuts through her like a dull knife, bringing her back to the present. She sits up and wipes her eyes, then rummages through the piles on the desk. The room, once a vibrant reflection of Sarah, now resembles a fragile photograph fading in the sun. There's so much here that she doesn't know what to take. What would have meant the most to Sarah? What will mean the most to her?

She opens a drawer and finds it stuffed with more photos and letters. One letter catches her eye; it's on thick, cream-colored paper and has the logo of a prestigious archery academy at the top. She scans it quickly and her heart sinks. It's an acceptance letter, dated only days before Sarah's accident. Erica hadn't known she'd even applied.

A million what-ifs crash through her mind. What if Sarah had told her about the application? What if she started at a new school and Erica never saw her again? What if Erica had been a better friend, more supportive, less consumed with her own rising stardom?

She stuffs the letter back in the drawer, angry at herself for the rising jealousy she feels. Even now, knowing everything, a part of her envies Sarah's talent. Her steadiness. Her potential. No, not just her potential, but everything she's already achieved.

Erica stands and looks around the room one last time. The archery set in the corner catches her eye: a sleek composite bow with a quiver full of arrows, all lovingly maintained. She walks over and runs her hand along the curve of the bow. It was Sarah's pride and joy, a gift from her grandparents. She knows how much the sport meant to Sarah, how every hour spent practicing was an investment in her future.

A surge of something—determination, maybe—swells inside her. This is more than just a piece of sporting equipment; it's a symbol of Sarah's dedication and passion. It's a part of her.

Erica lifts the bow from its stand and tests the weight in her hands. She remembers the first time she held a bow, how awkward and heavy it was. This one is different. It balances perfectly. The feeling is almost seductive, like the promise of a new ability.

"I'll take care of it," she says aloud, as if speaking to Sarah. "I'll take care of everything."

She imagines herself at the range, the target a distant blur. In her mind, she draws the bowstring back, notes the tension in her adjusted muscles, and releases. The arrow flies straight and true, piercing the center of the target with a satisfying thud.

The vision gives her a sense of purpose. She's always relied on her enhancements, on the easy fixes that the nanites provide. But maybe there's something to be gained from working toward a goal the old-fashioned way, from earning it through effort and persistence. Just like she did to make it onto the cheer team.

Erica takes a deep breath and makes her vow. "I promise to honor you, Sarah. To carry on our dreams and make you proud."

The weight of the bow in her hands feels significant, like a physical manifestation of her new commitment. For the first time in months, the path ahead becomes clear. It won't be easy, and it won't be quick, but she's willing to put in the work.

Before she leaves the room, she catches sight of a stack of books on a small shelf above Sarah's bed. Poetry books. Every poetry book Erica gave her over the years. She can't bear to open them now. Doesn't have the emotional stamina to flick through the meaningful pages, but she collects all the books under her other arm and takes them with her. Sarah will not be forgotten. Sarah will be remembered. Immortalized. If it's the last thing Erica does.

CHAPTER 10

Erica stands in the middle of the abandoned football field, a lone figure in the early morning mist. She notches an arrow, draws back the bowstring, and releases. The arrow slices through the air and buries itself in the target's bullseye with a dull thud. A small, satisfied smile curls on her lips, but her mood remains somber, lost in memories.

The sun stretches lazily over the horizon, casting long shadows that flicker and dance across the dewy grass. Erica retrieves her arrows, fingers tracing the fletching with a delicate reverence. Each one is like a fragile glass shard, a piece of something more significant than herself.

She remembers the first time she watched Sarah shoot. It was during a summer camp six years ago, before everything changed. Sarah had made it look so easy, pulling the string back with a confident grace and letting the arrow fly as if it were an extension of her own will. Erica had been in awe, not just of Sarah's skill, but of the serenity that enveloped her when she held the bow.

Now, as Erica draws another arrow and takes aim, she hopes to capture even a fragment of that same serenity. The bow hums with tension, her fingers burn with anticipation, and she releases. Another bullseye. The satisfaction is immediate but fleeting, like a sugar rush that leaves her more hollow than before.

Practicing archery isn't about learning a new skill; it's a way for Erica to connect with Sarah's memory. Every shot is a silent conversation, a question-and-answer session with the past. Would Sarah be proud of her? Is she angry that Erica is still here, plodding along without her? These thoughts gnaw at Erica, but she pushes them aside. She needs this. She needs to believe this practice is a tribute, not an appropriation.

The paper of the target rustles in the morning breeze, and Erica wipes her brow. The physicality of archery is more intense than she expected. Her arms ache, her shoulders scream in protest, her wings droop an exhausted coffee brown, but there's a masochistic pleasure in the pain. It reminds her she's alive, that she can still feel something.

A bird caws from the bleachers, a solitary fan in nature's grandstand. Erica glances over and imagines the stands filled with people, all of them there to support her in this quiet endeavor. It's a ridiculous thought; archery is one of the loneliest sports. That's part of its appeal. There's no team to fail, no partner to blame. Just a girl, a bow, and a target.

The empty field holds a thousand ghosts of high school memories. She thinks about the football games from the time before, how she and Jess laughed and yelled themselves hoarse. That was before the fallout, before Sarah's death cleaved them into two unequal parts: Jess, who could still function, and Erica, who was left floundering in a sea of grief.

Erica notches another arrow and draws the bowstring to her cheek. The sun is full and blinding now, casting a golden halo around the target. She squints, focuses, and releases. The arrow zips through the air, a tiny missile of hope, and strikes the center with a precision that startles her. Perhaps she really does have a natural talent for it.

Her phone buzzes in her backpack. She lets it go to voice-mail, already knowing it's her mom. "Erica, honey, we're worried about you. Call us back." Her parents mean well, but they can't understand why she'd rather spend her mornings here than at home or with friends. They think she's wallow-ing, that she's stuck. Maybe she is, but this is a rut she needs to ride out on her own terms.

The mornings are her favorite time to practice. The world is still half-asleep. She pretends she's the only person alive, that all the hurt and confusion are on pause. Once the day fully wakes, the illusion shatters, and she's thrust back into a reality she's not ready to face.

She retrieves her arrows again, savoring the short walk to the target and back. Each arrow is a mini-victory, a token of progress. She runs her fingers along the bow, remembering how awkward it felt in her hands at first. Now it fits her like a well-worn glove, like something meant for her all along.

The idea of competition flits through her mind. Could she be good enough to win something? She dismisses the idea as quickly as it came. It's not about winning or proving herself. It's about finding a way to survive, to hold on to the pieces of Sarah that are slipping through her fingers like whispers from a dying star.

Erica takes a deep breath and expels it slowly, drawing the bowstring back one more time. Her muscles scream in rebellion, but she ignores them. The tension in the string mirrors the tension in her life, taut and threatening to snap. She holds her breath, aims, and releases. The arrow flies true, sinking into the bullseye with a satisfying thud.

The birds scatter, and the world wakes as she notches another arrow.

She passes many months like this, the days slipping by like the incessant scroll of her EvolveMe feed, each day a repetitive yet comforting sequence for Erica. She wakes early, practices at the football field, goes to class, walks her way through cheer practice with her head in a cloud, then goes to the archery range in the next town over. Sarah wouldn't want her to quit cheer. Sarah would want her to follow her dreams. The problem is, Erica doesn't know what her dreams are any more. So she goes through the motions, earning herself the head cheerleader title, faking her smiles and interest. But the whole time, the only thing she can think about is how long it will be until she can get to the range.

This routine has become her lifeline.

)(X)(X)(X(

Erica sits in the locker room, the smell of sweat and old gym bags hanging heavy in the air. Her cheerleading uniform lies in a crumpled heap beside her, and she rubs her sore ankles. The last pep rally of the semester was particularly intense, with the squad practicing nonstop for a week. She should be relieved it's over, but instead, a different kind of weight presses on her chest.

"Erica, you coming?" One of the girls—she thinks it's Mercedes, but all their voices have started to blur together—pokes her head around the corner.

"Yeah, just a sec," Erica says, not moving.

Mercedes shrugs and skips off, the sound of her flip-flops echoing against the tiled walls. The rest of the team is planning to hit the new frozen yogurt place, eager to celebrate the national ward they won last week. They'll probably end up at someone's house with an illegal keg and a bunch of black market nanites. Erica knows she should go, that it would be the "team captain" thing to do, but the idea of spending another minute in their company makes her stomach twist.

She picks up her uniform and stuffs it into her locker, then closes the door with a soft click. The metal is cool against her forehead as she leans into it, eyes shut tight. She remembers how excited she was when she made the squad in freshman year. It seemed like the pinnacle of high school life: the tight-knit group of friends, the adoration of the student body, the endless social events. Now it's all so pointless. Hollow. Irrelevant. She's been playing the part for too many years.

Walking to the parking lot, she digs her keys from her backpack and looks over at the team. They're laughing and shouting, already high on sugar and camaraderie. She starts to wave, then changes her mind and heads for her car. The old second-hand driverless car was a hand-me-down from her brother, and it's seen better days. She loves it, though, if only because it gives her an escape.

As she settles into the back seat, thoughts of Sarah infiltrate her mind. They were such a balanced duo: Sarah, the sensible one and Erica, the ambitious, impulsive one. And then there is Jess. Who she still sees every day. Twice if there's cheer practice. Sarah was always so kind to her. Accepting their relationship without question. Without Sarah, her balance is thrown completely off, and Erica still isn't sure how to find her footing. Nothing exists between them except awkward glances and stiff shoulders.

She pulls into the archery range's gravel lot and kills the engine. The range is her favorite place in the world. It's quiet, except for the occasional twang of bowstrings and the soft chatter of birds. She likes to come here after school, to unwind and practice in a setting that's more legitimate than the makeshift field.

Inside, she waves to Ron, the grizzled old range master. He raises an eyebrow. "Thought you'd be at your celebration," he says. "Didn't you just win nationals?"

"I'll head there soon," she lies. "There's only so much post win chatter I can take."

Ron shrugs and goes back to fiddling with a compound bow. "Well, you know you're always welcome here."

Erica rents a lane and changes into her spare clothes: a comfortable pair of jeans and an old T-shirt of her brother's. She ties her hair back and examines her hands. The calluses are as part of her as her pom-poms, hard little islands of skin that mark her progress. She likes the way they feel, likes what they represent.

She sets up her gear and notches an arrow, taking her time with the first shot. The bow is an old friend now, her best friend. She releases, and the arrow kisses the target's center with a familiarity that's almost boring. She doesn't need to check; she knows it was a perfect shot.

The thing is, she's getting too good. Without a challenge, the practice feels like going through the motions. That's why she considered entering a competition, to see where she stands against real opponents. But in the end, she decided against it. Competing would make it something else, something more than a personal tribute. It would make it about her, and that would be wrong.

She draws and releases another arrow, then another, each one finding its mark with mechanical precision. The repetition frees her mind to wander. She thinks about the message she sent to the cheer deputy captain, about how quitting the squad will give her more time for archery. She doesn't dare tell them she thinks the whole thing is shallow and pointless; that would be cruel. But she can't keep pretending that it means something to her anymore.

In her mind, she replays the scene with Jess from yesterday. They ran into each other at the grocery store, in the cereal aisle of all places. For a moment, Erica thought Jess was going to talk to her, that maybe they could reconcile. But Jess merely gave a tight-lipped smile and walked away. That hurt more than if she'd said something nasty. Something she deserved.

Erica finishes her set and retrieves the arrows. The range is nearly empty, and she likes it that way. She wonders how long she can keep this up, doing it all alone. Can she get better without a coach, without any kind of feedback? Does it even matter?

Reluctantly, she packs her gear away. The idea of going home and facing her mom, who will undoubtedly ask how the "celebration" was, fills her with dread. She likes it here, in this unremarkable space where she doesn't have to answer to anyone.

The range has become her sanctuary, a place where she can be alone with her thoughts and her bow, where she can uncover who she really is.

CHAPTER 11

High school hallways are their own kind of battleground, and Erica has learned to navigate them with the skill of a seasoned soldier. Lockers clang like makeshift weapons, and the roar of a thousand conversations creates an ever-present din. In this chaotic terrain, she knows how to find the quiet spots, the neutral zones where she can take a breath and plan her next move.

One such spot is the drinking fountain near the art room. It's recessed, giving it a tranquil, almost zen-like quality. Erica takes a slow sip, then another, letting the cold water trickle down her throat and cool her from the inside out. She checks her watch; she's in no hurry to get to English class, where they're slogging through yet another dystopian novel. The future is bleak enough without adding fictional despair to the mix.

As she turns to leave, she sees Jess. She stands along the hall, talking to a girl from the swim team. Erica can't remember her name, but she knows she's a junior, and the way they are looking at each other reveals they are more than friends. The thought should make her happy for Jess, but all she feels is a dull, grinding envy. Not because she wants the girl, or Jess back, but because she wants what Jess has: the ability to move on.

The bell rings, and the crowd surges into the hallways. Erica walks away, then slows, her feet dragging on the linoleum. She risks a glance over her shoulder and sees Jess weaving through the mass of bodies, heading in her direction. Her heart quickens, not with fear, but with a desperate hope. Maybe Jess will say something. Maybe they can clear the air.

"Erica," Jess says, closing the gap.

Erica stops and turns, bracing herself. "Hey."

"You quit the squad?"

The question isn't accusatory, but Erica detects a note of genuine confusion, perhaps even concern. She hesitates, searching Jess' face for clues. It's a face she knows better than her own, yet it feels like staring into a stranger's eyes.

"I just...needed more time for other things," Erica says, avoiding specifics. She's not ready to explain her obsession with archery, or how she thinks it's saving her in a way that cheer never could.

Jess nods, her expression unreadable. "We could have used you for the last game. It's not the same without you."

A rush of conflicting emotions hits Erica. She wants to yell at Jess for making her feel guilty, for acting like everything is fine when it's so clearly not. But she also wants to thank her, to cry and say she's sorry for every unkind word, for every moment of distance she's created.

"I'm sorry," Erica says, though even she's not sure what she's apologizing for. Maybe for all of it. Maybe for nothing.

"Yeah," Jess says, then adds, "It's just that—never mind."

Erica waits, hoping Jess will finish the thought, will tell her how she really feels, will give her something to work with. But Jess shrugs and walks away.

"Jess, wait," Erica calls, her voice cracking.

Jess pauses, half-turning, a flicker of expectation in her eyes. She takes a step toward her, then another, closing the distance to a manageable gap.

"I'm glad you're doing okay," Erica says, and she means it, though the words come out more resigned than she intended.

Jess gives a small, sad smile. "Thanks."

With that, Jess disappears into the throng of students, leaving Erica standing alone and static in the moving crowd. She knows she could have said more, should have said more, but the fear of rejection holds her tongue.

She thinks back to the day after Sarah's death, when she and Jess had their big fight. It wasn't even about Sarah; it was about them, about how Jess expected Erica to be the same person she was before, when all Erica wanted was to dissolve into the background and not exist for a while. In that moment, she hated Jess for her strength, for her ability to keep going, for her sense of right and wrong.

Now she sees that strength as something different, something more fragile. A façade, maybe, or a coping mechanism. She wonders if Jess is as broken as she is, and if that's why they can't be together any more—because seeing each other is like looking in a cracked mirror.

Erica arrives at her English classroom and lingers by the

door. Her class is already seated, the teacher is droning on about themes and symbolism. She doesn't have the energy for it. Not today.

She turns and heads for the nearest exit, thinking about the range, about how many arrows she has left in her quiver. The warm spring air hits her as she leaves the school, tempting her to fly away and be free of all this. Maybe she will.

Her dreams are full of wings and feathers. And the next day, Erica sits alone in the cafeteria, picking at a salad that looks more like a compost heap than a meal. She's never been a huge fan of vegetables, but since she stopped eating lunch with the cheer squad, she's had to make concessions. The salad bar is the only part of the lunchroom she can navigate without feeling like an intruder.

She glances over to where the squad usually sits. Today they're mixed in with the soccer team, creating a writhing mass of athletic pecking order. In the center of it all is Jess, her wings loud and proud, laughing at something one boy says. Erica can't help but notice how the lines of stress and fatigue melt away from Jess' face when she laughs. It's the kind of laugh that makes others join in, even if they don't know what's funny.

With a sigh, Erica stabs a wilted piece of lettuce and brings it to her lips, then drops it back into the bowl, defeated. Her eyes wander to the line for the pizza counter, and she spots him: Joe Rucker. He's tall, recently took a bulk nanite, and has filled out handsomely. His hair is a tousled mess of corn-colored waves, perpetually in need of a cut, and his smile—God, that smile—can light up even the dreariest biology class.

Joe used to have a crush on Sarah, but now he is talking to Heather, another girl on the cheerleading team. He's moved on. Why can't Erica? Their eyes meet, and there is a flash of something, a quickening of her pulse, a flush of heat to her cheeks, but Erica buries it deep. Joe is not for her. She doesn't deserve him. She doesn't deserve anyone.

Joe and Heather flirt, their interactions a well-rehearsed dance of intimacy. Heather pokes Joe in his unbreakable ribs, and he feigns injury, wrapping her in a playful headlock. Erica's chest tightens with a mix of envy and longing. It's not that she wants Joe; she wants what they have. The easy affection, the companionship. Someone to hold her steady when she is tipping over the edge.

Her phone buzzes in her backpack. She fishes it out and finds a text from her mom: "Don't forget, Dr. Klein at 4pm." Wonderful. She'd managed to block out the fact that she has to see her therapist today. Dr. Klein is nice enough, but Erica hates talking about her feelings. She'd much rather shoot arrows at a target and let her mind go blank.

The phone goes back in the pack, and she returns her gaze to Joe and Heather. They've procured their slices and are making their way to an open table. Heather spots Erica and waves enthusiastically. Erica's first instinct is to look away, to pretend she didn't see, but it's too late. She forces a smile and lifts her hand in a half-hearted wave.

"Erica! Come join us!" Heather calls.

Erica hesitates. She knows if she says no, Heather will come over and drag her to the table anyway. If she says yes, she'll have to endure the painful sweetness of watching the two lovebirds canoodle. It's a lose-lose situation, but she calculates that complying will be the less excruciating option.

She stands and walks over, carrying her sad excuse for a salad. Heather scoots her chair closer to Joe, making space for Erica to sit. The three of them form a crooked triangle.

"How's practice going?" Heather asks, not specifying which practice. That used to be a dangerous question, as Erica was always juggling multiple activities. Now, the answer is simple.

"Good," Erica says. "I'm getting better."

Joe leans in, curious. "What are you practicing these days? I heard you quit the cheer squad."

"Archery," Erica says, watching Joe's face for a reaction. "It's more my speed right now."

"That's badass," Joe says, and Erica's heart does a little somersault. "Do you have one of those cool wrist guards and everything?"

"Yeah," she says, a tiny spark of pride igniting. "I have my own bow too."

Joe nods, clearly impressed. "Would you show me sometime? I've always wanted to try it."

A thousand scenarios flash through Erica's mind: her teaching Joe how to hold the bow, their hands touching, him looking at her the way she looks at him. Then Heather, in one swift stroke, ruins her daydream by saying, "I'd love to watch."

Of course she would. Erica swallows and forces another smile. "Sure. Anytime."

The conversation drifts to safer topics—college plans, summer jobs—and Erica mostly listens, occasionally chiming in with a noncommittal "yeah" or "cool." They tell her Joe has been drafted to the NFL, that Heather plans to major in journalism. She already knows these things, but hearing them again solidifies the reality that their lives are moving forward while she is stuck in place.

The lunch period winds down and students trickle out of the cafeteria. Erica checks her watch, noting that if she skips class, she has enough time for a practise session before heading to Dr. Klein's. She makes her excuses when Heather says, "Hey, we should all hang out after graduation. Like, the whole gang."

Erica freezes. The "whole gang" probably means the entire cheerleading and football team.

"Yeah," Erica says slowly. "That'd be nice."

Heather beams, and Erica wonders if she really believes that, or if she's playing a role, trying to maintain the fiction that they'll all remain friends after graduation. Erica can't think of a single person she'll stay in touch with. It's time to reinvent herself. Start fresh. College is the perfect opportunity to do that.

The three of them stand, and Erica feels a sinking in her gut, like the last moments of a rollercoaster ride that drops you straight into reality. She turns to go, but Joe touches her arm, stopping her.

"Erica," he says, and her name in his voice sends a shiver down her spine. "I'm serious about the archery. Let me know when."

She nods, unable to speak, and walks away, leaving the two of them to their happiness. Her heart is as heavy as her unspoken words.

CHAPTER 12

GRADUATION STEAMS closer with more insistence than a freight train. On the big day, the auditorium is a sea of blue caps and gowns, the air thick with the heady mix of accomplishment and anxiety about the future. Erica sits toward the back, her chin buried in her cloak, the new HoloGems her parents bought her in her ears and projecting scenes of butterflies wearing little mortarboards. The principal drones through the list of names, and each one is met with a chorus of cheers and the occasional air horn blast. When she gets to "Erica Swiftfield," Erica stands, walks to the stage, and accepts her diploma with a practiced smile. Her parents holler from the balcony, and she gives them a small, grateful wave.

The ceremony grinds to a close, and the newly minted graduates explode into the parking lot, a mass of blue fabric and hugging bodies. Erica finds her family, and her mom pulls her into a tight embrace.

"We're so proud of you," her mom says, tears already streaming.

"Thanks, Mom." Erica extracts herself gently and turns to her dad, who's holding a bouquet of daisies.

"Thought you might like these," he says.

Erica takes the flowers, their scent bursting like summer in her nose. "They're perfect," she says, though she knows she'll only leave them in the car to wilt. She's no good at taking care of things.

"Let's take some pictures," her mom says, already digging in her purse for the camera.

They snap a few traditional shots—Erica with her diploma, Erica with her parents, Erica pretending to throw her cap in the air—but all Erica wants to do is go home and curl up in her bed.

She waves off the invites to parties, the camping trip to the lake, the vacation to Heather's summer cabin, and spends the next week at home. Every single daylight hour that crawls by during the long summer days she spends at the range until her muscles harden and accommodate her new routine.

During the third week, she has to explain to her parents that she didn't get her college applications in on time. They insist she get a job.

In the fourth week, her parents make her sit with them and complete college applications for the following year. Erica's heart isn't in it, but what else will she do?

She gets a job working at the diner where she and Jess and Sarah shared slushies all those years ago. She feels closer to Sarah here. Sometimes Mai comes in and orders a slushy.

She's not sure Mai remembers her, but she always gives her an extra large, no matter what she pays for.

On the fifth week she watches Joe Rucker on TV crushing it in the NFL.

At the end of the summer, everyone leaves for college and Erica is alone. Exactly how she wants it. She spends a few days touring Adjusted Athletics looking at the newest nanites, wondering if there's something that might take her grief away. Or at the very least, help her feel something other than this gaping sadness.

She doesn't see anyone at Thanksgiving. Jason comes home for the weekend. He's a full-fledged marine now. There's a new sparkle in his eyes. An unnatural sparkle. Erica suspects he's been given a nanite of some kind. Most soldiers these days have bulked up. It's only a matter of time before Jason follows suit.

Christmas is without Jason as he's been deployed. She doesn't meet with any high school friends home from college, not unless they eat at the diner. Joe comes in one day a couple of days before Christmas, looking for the gift box of pastries they make. His smile stretches when he sees her behind the counter.

"Erica! How are things? Still shooting?"

He remembers. "Yeah. Everyday. Thanks for asking. Looks like you've been killing it on the field."

A blush colors his cheeks. He leans over the counter. "Between you and me, I'm not sure how I feel about all the attention."

Erica's lips twitch. "Rookie of the Year isn't good enough for you?"

"Oh, it's exactly what I wanted," he says as he selects his pastries. "I love signing autographs in the street. But the girls..." he shakes his head.

"There's no law against threesomes you know." Erica laughs.

Joe's color deepens and he shakes his head. "I'm a one-woman kind of guy. And I need to focus on my career, not get distracted by long legs and short skirts."

Erica pats his hand. Beneath Joe's good looks and affable nature, is a serious person with their head screwed on right. "I get that."

He looks up and their gazes collide. "I'd still like to watch you shoot. You free after Christmas?"

Erica nods. It's the first time someone has shown interest in being her friend in years.

But Christmas passes and Joe is called back early for a holiday game. Erica watches it on TV. By January she's pretty much given up on her EvolveMe feed. Her BioTunes playlist no longer centers her. And by March, both pairs of HoloGem earrings are in the trash, along with her WingCam, which has become nothing more than a dust catcher. She holds onto the purple sweater Sarah gave her. She never got it altered. Erica raises the soft material to her face and brushes it against her cheek. It's never been worn, but she can somehow smell Sarah on it.

Later in February, she reads Joe Rucker endured a life-changing injury on the field and will never play football again. Unless he gets a regeneration nanite, which his team is refusing to provide him with. Anger seethes under the surface for him. She was offered a few cheer scholarships to college, and all of them came with regeneration nanites in the insurance policy. Wings are delicate. They get ripped all the time. And the brutal nature of the flip combinations often result in broken wing bones. But Erica's never heard of a bulk being injured. Assumes it's not part of a regular football insurance policy. She sends Joe a heartfelt message, but he doesn't reply. She doesn't blame him.

By April, Erica accrues the most hours in the range of all time, earning herself a special discount. She doesn't want it. Just wants to shoot, but Ron insists, so she smiles and thanks him politely.

At the beginning of May, Erica contemplates flying away. She doesn't know where. Maybe to see something new. Anything to get out of this town and feel a different emotion. She has accepted one of the scholarship offers to a state college, but she has no intention of actually attending. She wishes it was for archery, but there is no way she'll ever use her talent for gain. Her thoughts are interrupted when her brother calls one night during dinner.

Her mom thumbs her phone. "He wants to video call."

They crowd around the phone. Jason's face pops onto the screen, grinning from ear to ear.

"Little sis! Congrats on the scholarship!" he says, and Erica's heart warms. Jason has been stationed overseas for months, and she misses him more than she realized.

"Thanks, Jase. How's it going?"

They chat for a bit, with Jason telling stories about his latest adventures and asking Erica about her plans for the summer. She keeps her answers vague; working at the diner doesn't provide her with the best anecdotes.

Just as they're about to sign off, Jason says, "Oh, have you guys seen the news? Big announcement from President Bear."

Her dad perks up. "What's he said now?"

Jason's face grows serious. "He's making it mandatory for all unadjusteds to take a nanite. Says it's for the good of the nation."

Erica's stomach drops. "Are you kidding?"

"I wish. Go check it out. Love you guys." With that, the call ends.

Her parents exchange looks.

Erica remembers the first time she learned about nanites in biology class. The tiny, programmable pills were hailed as the next big thing, able to alter a person's DNA with surgical precision. Want to be taller? Smarter? More attractive? There is a nanite for that. The adjusted population skyrocketed within a few years, with most people treating it like upgrading an app on their phone.

Her parents go to the living room, calling to Erica to join them. The three of them stand in front of the TV and watch the announcement on its fiftieth reiteration. The familiar logo of the Adjusted News Network spins in the corner, and a blonde, overly-symmetrical anchor reads from her teleprompter.

"Earlier today, President Bear issued an executive order requiring all unadjusteds to take a nanite within the next year. Citing public health and economic stability, the President emphasized this move is necessary to ensure a more equal and efficient society. Let's take a look at his statement."

The screen cuts to a podium, where President Bear stands in his trademark intimation stance. Erica doesn't like the man, but seeing him in high definition makes her loathe him even more. His eyes are red, his hulking mass almost as large as a bulk.

"This is a national announcement. All unadjusteds age twelve and over will now be required to take a nanite to enhance their abilities. With threats and competition from overseas, we must do more to further the strength of our country."

Erica's hands clench into fists. She can feel her pulse in her temples, a rapid, angry drumbeat.

"The nanite representative agency is on its way to every school right now. They will assign each eligible unadjusted a ticket number. You are not permitted to leave before you have your ticket. This ticket will tell you which day within the next two weeks you will be assessed for an appropriate nanite level. You'll notice some of those assessments start today. Nanite reps and soldiers are on their way to each school in every city to aid the process. Once this assessment is complete, we will proceed to residences to evaluate the unadjusted adults. I expect each unadjusted individual to join the strength of the adjusted superbeings. Failure to comply will result in unfortunate circumstances."

The feed cuts back to the anchor, who summarizes the decree in a chirpy, unbothered tone. Erica can't hear her; her mind is stuck on Bear's words, on the cold, calculated logic of them.

Her dad mutes the TV. "This is bad," he says, looking at Erica.

"Yeah," she says, her voice hollow. She is the only one in the family who is adjusted.

Her mom shifts uncomfortably. "Maybe it won't be as drastic as it sounds. There could be exemptions, or—"

"Or maybe we'll all fall in line like good little citizens," her dad interrupts. "This is how it starts, you know."

Erica's eyes dart between her parents. "You mean...you guys aren't going to take one?"

Her dad leans back in his chair, crossing his arms. "We've gotten along fine without them so far."

"We?" her mom says, eyebrows raised. "I could finally get those wings I've been coveting."

"They'd look good on you," Erica says, but inside, her stomach is a mass of coiling snakes. What if she has a reaction, like Sarah? They can't do this. President Bear can't do this.

"I guess increased processing skills could help me in the office," her dad says.

Erica can't believe they are considering it. But what is the alternative? "Unfortunate circumstances" isn't a term President Bear uses lightly. And what about Jason? What ability will they force on him overseas? Will they turn all soldiers into bulks with impenetrable skin?

Erica stands, the tension in the room too much for her. "I need to go to Dr. Klein's."

Her mom gives her a sympathetic look. "I hope it helps, sweetheart."

"Thanks, Mom." Erica touches her shoulder as she walks by. She grabs the car keys and heads for the door, leaving her parents in a confused, concerned silence.

The car reverses out of the driveway, heading toward the main road. Her mind races with the implications of Bear's decree. It's not just about taking a nanite; it's about conformity, about losing what makes you uniquely you. She thinks of the adjusteds: people with wings or horns or tails, the same confident glint in their eyes, the lavish nature of their enhancements. They are a populace crafted from a single mold, an army of attractive, efficient drones. They look like her. Or she looks like them.

The archery range comes into view. The car parks in the gravel lot and the engine cuts off. Erica stares at the entrance. She's got a bit of time before her session with Dr. Klein.

She walks into the range, the familiar smell of wood calming her immediately. Ron looks up from the front desk, his perpetual scowl softening when he sees her.

"Ever thought about entering a competition?" he says, respect in his eyes. "We run them here sometimes. I can show you the entry form?"

Erica shakes her head and her wings turn a sad pale blue. "I don't want to compete."

"Suit yourself."

Erica walks along her assigned lane, then turns back to ask Ron a question. "Hey, Ron? Are you unadjusted?"

He nods.

"What will you take?"

He shrugs. "Whatever the give me, I guess. I hear we have to pay for most of it, and I can't afford much..." he splays a hand. "So it won't be higher than class three."

"I'm sorry," she says.

He waves a hand, but she notes the tension bracketing his eyes and mouth. "We need to do what we need to do to make this country great again."

"Yeah." Erica bites her lip. Now is not the time to get into a political argument, especially when she suspects Ron wants nothing to do with nanites. But what choice does he have? You either embrace it or...face *unfortunate circumstances*. Erica remembers when one of the lead scientists of the nanite program refused to make any more. She got thrown into prison for her trouble. She's still there. If she hasn't been quietly killed.

With her heart heavy, Erica heads to her assigned lane. The bow feels like lead in her hands today, like it's absorbing all the weight of her worries. She notches an arrow, takes aim, and releases. The arrow wobbles in flight and sticks in the outer ring of the target. She curses under her breath.

Erica retrieves the arrow and tries again, this time taking longer to steady her grip and control her breathing. The shot is better, landing in the third ring, but still far from her usual accuracy. Her mind is too cluttered, her emotions too raw.

She thinks about the unadjusted who have resisted so far. Many of them are like her family: people who value their natural selves, who believe in the strength of their unadjusted genetics. What will they do now? Can they really stand against a presidential mandate?

And what about herself? Where does she stand? What should she do?

Her thoughts swirl around Joe, around Heather, around her parents and Jess. Around Sarah. Erica has taken three nanites. And she wanted each one. It was her choice. But she wouldn't force it on anyone. Not again.

Erica packs away her gear, her hands moving on autopilot. A somber quiet fills the empty space of the range. She likes to think every arrow she's ever shot has left a mark some-where in these walls, that they've created a framework of her history, each one telling a small part of her story.

She walks back to her car and sits in front, not turning the engine on. Her phone buzzes; it's her mom, probably wondering where she is. She lets it go to voicemail and leans back, closing her eyes.

President Bear's words play on a loop in her head: "This is not just about enhancement; it is about survival." She knows he's right, in a twisted sort of way. The adjusted are stronger, more capable. In a world that prizes efficiency above all else, they have a clear advantage.

But where does that leave the unadjusteds? Where does that leave her?

Taking a stand could cost her everything, but doing nothing would cost her even more.

She makes it to Dr. Klein's appointment, but doesn't take anything in. Stares out the window the entire time, the doctor's voice coming to her like it's underwater. Has the doctor taken a nanite? If she has, Erica can't tell by looking at her. She has no idea how the doctor feels about President Bear's new mandate.

The car drives Erica home on autopilot. Erica eats dinner on autopilot. Scrolls through her socials on autopilot. Then she falls asleep.

She wakes to the sound of birds chirping outside her window. She's transported back to simpler times—summer vacations, carefree weekends—when the morning chorus was something to look forward to. Now it feels intrusive, like nature is mocking her with its unearned optimism.

She rolls over and checks her phone. Twenty new messages in the group chat for her graduating class. It petered out months ago. But today, someone has posted a screenshot of an article with the headline: "President Bear's Nanite Mandate: A New Age of Equality?" The accompanying text is a flurry of opinions, most of them in support of the decree. Erica closes the app, not wanting to see who's written what. She has a pretty good idea.

Her phone buzzes. It's Heather: "Bear is totally right. It's about time everyone got on the same level."

Erica's hand tightens around the phone. Heather's adjusted parents gave her every advantage since middle school. She is taller, more coordinated, even eerily symmetrical, not to mention the enormous swan wings. Of course she thinks the mandate is a good thing. In her world, being adjusted is the baseline.

She types a response: "Yeah, it's insane." Then deletes it. Types: "People should have a choice." Deletes that too. Finally, she writes: "IDK" and sends it. She's not ready to alienate Heather, not yet. But can she convince her to see things differently?

With a groan, Erica gets out of bed and heads to the kitchen. Her dad is already at work, but her mom sits at the table, sipping coffee and reading the newspaper on her tablet.

"Morning," her mom says, putting down her mug. "We need to talk."

Erica's shoulders tense. "About what?"

Her mom folds the paper neatly, then pauses, as if weighing her words on an invisible scale. "About yesterday. I know you're worried. Because of what happened to Sarah. But your father and I don't have a choice—"

"There is always a choice!" The banked anger erupts out of Erica, surprising her.

"And then what?" Her mom splays a hand. "We go on the run? Where? The tracking drones would corner us in minutes."

Erica sinks into the opposite chair. "I don't know. But I don't want this for you."

Her mom puts a hand over hers. "Let's not panic until we're assessed. Until we know more. It might not be as bad as you think. It could be something small, like a permanent tan—"

Erica scoffs. President Bear wants to further the country, not make everyone look pretty.

"I know it's been hard for you since Sarah's death. I know you blame yourself." Her mom's eyes roam over Erica's face. "But we're not going anywhere. It's going to be okay."

Erica shakes her head. "You don't know that."

There is nothing more to say, nothing more to be done, so Erica leaves her mom to her cooling coffee and trudges back to her room, her wings trailing behind her. They're too much effort to expand.

She thinks about the adjusteds and the unadjusteds, about choice and conformity. About how every decision she's made in the past year was an attempt to hold on to who she is, to who Sarah was. Can she still be herself if she lets this happen? But what can one nineteen-year-old do against a presidential order?

Her eyes land on her laptop, and she remembers the

article Heather sent. With a reluctance born of duty, she opens her class's group chat and scrolls through the messages until she finds the link.

The article is on a popular news site, one that bills itself as cutting-edge but reads like an industry newsletter for the adjusted elite. The author makes a passionate case for the mandate, arguing that the unadjusteds are a drag on society, that they're holding back progress. "In a world where everyone can be their best selves, why cling to mediocrity?" the article asks. "The nanites do not erase who you are; they simply unlock your potential."

Erica closes her laptop, hard, and sits back in her chair. The words swirl in her mind: "holding back progress," "clinging to mediocrity," "unlock your potential." She knows propaganda when she sees it.

Her phone buzzes again, and this time she dreads looking at it. When she does, her heart skips. It's Jess.

"Can we talk?" the message reads. "About the mandate."

Erica's mind races. Why would Jess want to talk to her about this? They're not even speaking. But then she remembers that Jess' mom is unadjusted, and a possible rift between the family makes sense.

She types: "Sure. When?"

"Now? I'm outside."

Erica's breath catches. She goes to her window and peeks through the blinds. Sure enough, Jess is in her driveway, sitting on the hood of her car. She looks at her phone and sees the outline of a new message forming, then the words: "Please."

A hundred reasons to say no flood Erica's mind, but one

simple yes overrides them all. She needs an ally, someone who understands, and maybe—just maybe—this could bring them back together.

She texts: "Coming," and heads for the door.

Outside, the air is warm and thick with the promise of summer. Erica trudges down the path, each step a tentative probe into the minefield of their fractured friendship. Jess watches her approach, her eyes shielded by oversized sunglasses that make her look like an insect with her large, orange wings on display. She looks older, more mature, more confident, more beautiful. Everything Erica is not. She hasn't seen her since graduation, but she keeps an eye on her through EvovleMe, in a non-stalker kind of way.

"Hey," Jess says, sliding off the car, bringing with her the familiar scent of her coconut shampoo.

"Hey," Erica replies, stopping a few feet away. "Are you back for the summer?"

Jess nods. "Three months of Wichita fun."

"How's it been?"

A tense smile forms on Jess' face. "Good. Fun. I love it. The cheer team is awesome."

She is lying, but Erica doesn't know why. An awkward silence envelops them, the kind that comes from too many unspoken words and unhealed wounds.

"I didn't come here to talk about school." Jess' hands wind into her shirt. "I'm freaking out about the mandate. If anyone understands, I reckon you do. What are we supposed to do?"

Erica isn't sure if Jess means her family or humanity in general. "Resist? Adapt? I don't know. It's insane."

"Yeah, I knew you'd understand," Jess says, biting her lip. She takes off her sunglasses, and Erica sees the fear in her eyes, the same fear that's been gnawing at her. "Do you think they can really do this?"

Erica pulls at a hangnail on her thumb. "We are no longer living in a democracy."

"My mom is adjusted," Jess says, her voice small.

"When did that happen?"

"Las summer. Wings. So we could fly together."

Erica grimaces, remembering her own mother making the same suggestion. Erica wanted nothing to do with it. "Then what are you worrying about?"

"Because it's bigger than my mom and me. No one should be forced..."

They both wince at the word choice.

"No," Erica agrees, "no one should be forced."

A delicate silence falls between them

"They're disappearing," Jess says.

"Who are?"

"The unadjusteds. Some of them tried to run. Got rounded up and taken away. Nanite junkies are killing each other in the streets. Where have you been?"

Erica hasn't left her room since the announcement. She scans the street now, notes how unnaturally silent is.

"I'm going to fight." Erica says, her wings fluttering a bold blue. "They can't get away with this."

Jess gives her a once over. "I guess you can, with your archery skills. There's not much I can do with a couple of flips."

On impulse, Erica grabs both of Jess' hands, looking for

the girl who was once her closest confidante. She wants to believe that Jess is still the practical one, that she'll stand with her. "We have to do something."

"What?"

The two of them stand in the driveway, a fragile truce holding them together. A flicker of hope ignites in Erica's chest. Not just for herself, but for the unadjusteds, for humanity. Maybe they can resist. Maybe they can retain what makes them human.

"I don't know yet," Erica replies.

Jess nods and puts her sunglasses back on. "There's a hideout."

Erica frowns. "What kind of hideout?"

"I caught wind of a couple of unadjusteds talking. Addison, I think her name is." Erica remembers the tall, red-headed classmate. They were close friends in middle school. She hasn't spoken to her since she graduated. She hasn't spoken to anyone. "There's a place where they're all meeting. To hide. To resist."

"Where?"

Jess narrows her eyes.

Erica's frown deepens and her wings turn an acid green. "I want to help."

Jess expels a pent up breath. "Okay. Back toward Central City. In a cave in a valley in the middle of the woods." She gives her the coordinates and Erica commits them to memory. "They could use someone like you."

Someone like me. Erica doesn't know what that means. No one needs a person responsible for the death of their best friend on their team. She can't make things right with Sarah, can't bring her back from the dead, but she can prevent nanites from stealing more lives.

"Thank you," Erica says.

"Good luck."

"Aren't you going?"

Jess shakes her head. "I can't...I don't know how to fight."

A foreign sensation fills Erica's throat as she looks at her old friend. It takes her a minute to name it. Disappointment. She is disappointed in Jess. She always thought Jess was stronger than that.

"Stay safe," Erica says, finally closing the door on the hold Jess has over her.

As Jess gets into her car, Erica steps back toward her house. Jess pulls out of the driveway and onto the street, the car slowing briefly as if Jess is going to stop and say something more. But she doesn't, and the car accelerates away, leaving Erica standing on the warm asphalt with the burgeoning determination to fight.

CHAPTER 13

FOR THE FIRST time in a long while, Erica is moving forward. She is running toward something instead of away.

That night, after her parents go to bed, she opens her laptop and searches for the coordinates to the hideout. After planning a route, she deletes her search history. She's not stupid. She knows the country is about to blow up and she won't be responsible for bringing President Bear's army to the unadjusteds.

The thought of the hideout makes her heart race. She has wings. Will they accept her? Will they trust her?

Over the next few days, Erica prepares in secret. She buys a bus ticket from the station down the street, using cash to avoid leaving a trail. She goes to her nanite rep meeting, shows off her color-changing wings. They pass her with a big stamp and a beaming smile, as well as a digital passport she keeps on her phone. Then it is her parents' turn. Her mom gets wings. Her dad gets increased processing skills, as they both wanted. They are respected citizens. There is no reason not to grant them what they want. They both take the pills—handing over a large fee for the privilege at the same time—and adapt to the changes with no negative side effects. Then they go about their lives, ignoring the increasing violence among the more enhanced adjusteds, ignoring the unadjusteds being rounded up and held...somewhere...with increasing regularity, ignoring everything that is wrong with the world. For Erica, it's not enough.

She doesn't tell her parents about her plans, though the guilt weighs on her. How can she explain it? They'd try to talk her out of it, convince her staying here and complying is the smarter, safer option. Maybe they're right, but she believes in what she's doing.

The night before she's set to leave, Erica lies in bed, staring at the ceiling. Her room is a museum of her childhood, with DigiPosters of boy bands and famous cheerleaders flickering with age. She thinks about the dreams she had growing up: to be popular, to win competitions, to go to a good college. Dreams that now seem so small and replaceable.

Her eyes drift to the corner where Sarah's bow rests, propped up like an abandoned signpost on a deserted road. It is the one thing she hesitates to take. The bow is precious to her, not just as a memory of Sarah, but as an extension of her own will. Taking it means committing to this path, to this fight.

She gets out of bed and retrieves a duffel bag from her closet, then walks to the bow and runs her fingers along its curves. Gently, she lifts it and places it in the bag, along with a quiver of arrows. The rest of the bag is packed with clothes, a few toiletries, and one of the book of poems Sarah gave her.

Erica unzips the duffel and looks at its contents, imagining herself standing with other unadjusteds. She zips the bag closed, the sound slicing through the silent room, and sits on her bed, hugging the duffel to her chest.

What would Sarah think of all this? She thinks Sarah would tell her she's doing the right thing. But the truth is, Erica can barely remember who Sarah was. Who she _really_ was. Erica spent too much time absorbed in her own selfish dramas to understand who her best friend grew into. She unzips the duffel again and removes the book of poems. Flipping through the pages, she searches for a specific poem, one that meant a lot to them both. When she finds it, she traces the lines with her finger, reading them slowly. Tears well in her eyes, but she blinks them away. This is the path she's chosen, and she has to see where it leads. She closes the book and places it back in the duffel.

The clock on her nightstand reads 11:30 PM. She takes a deep breath, letting it fill her lungs and stretch her ribcage, then exhales. It's time.

Erica stands and slings the duffel over her shoulder. She opens her bedroom door, peering into the darkened hallway. The house is silent, her parents fast asleep. She tiptoes down the stairs and to the front door, where she slips on her shoes and grips the doorknob.

The cool night air hits her like a wake-up call. There is no turning back.

The streets are eerily quiet, the kind of silence that only small towns can produce in the dead of night. Erica marches along the sidewalk, clutching the duffel bag tight against her body. Each step echoes off the tarmac, creating a rhythm that competes with the pounding of her heart.

She's thankful for the warm night; it means fewer people will question her. A lone figure in a heavy coat walking at this hour might draw suspicion, but someone in a T-shirt and jeans could be taking a late-night stroll. At least, that's what she tells herself.

Her mind flicks through a slideshow of memories: walking these same streets with Sarah and Jess after school, laughing and eating ice cream; the first time Jess kissed her, just around the corner from her house; the night she and Sarah snuck out to see a meteor shower in the park. These streets are woven into the fabric of her life, and the thought of leaving them behind tugs at her more than she expected.

She arrives at the bus station and checks the time. She's early, but that's better than the alternative. The station is little more than a covered bench and a ticket kiosk, illuminated by a single, flickering streetlamp. It casts a jaundiced glow over the empty lot, giving the scene an otherworldly quality.

Erica sits on the bench and sets the duffel bag beside her, unzipping it enough to see the bow inside. She removes the book of poems and runs her fingers over the cover, remembering the day Sarah gave it to her. They'd been at the local bookstore, goofing around in the children's section, when Sarah grabbed the book from a bargain bin and thrust it into Erica's hands.

"You need some culture," Sarah said, grinning. "Plus, it has a really pretty cover."

Erica laughed, but when she opened the book and read

the first few lines, she knew it was something special. She still thinks the cover is gaudy, with its swirling pastel patterns and faux-leather texture, but the words inside have grown on her like a grafted piece of soul.

A car rounds the corner and drives along the street, its headlights washing over Erica and momentarily blinding her. She squints and raises a hand to shade her eyes, her body tensing with primal fear. But the car carries on down the street, turns the corner, and disappears.

A few minutes later, the bus pulls up, its engine purring as the doors whoosh open. Erica gives one last glance over her shoulder, grabs her duffel bag, then steps into the yawning entrance of the bus, wondering if this is when she disappears forever.

She flashes her ticket at the machine, which chirps at her and tells her to buckle up, then makes her way down the aisle, noting the few passengers inside are all obviously adjusted. Wings, tails, horns, a shimmering teleportation aura. Like her, they must all have the seal of approval from the Nanite Enforcement Agency on their phones.

Erica settles into a window seat toward the back, her duffel beside her, and watches the world go by as the bus ambles through deserted streets. She scrolls through her social feeds and gasps when she comes across a reward notice. A million each for Dr. Rufus Melody and his daughter Silver. Alive. Erica shakes her head, her chest pinching. It's hard enough to be on the run when no one is after you. But throw in the army, hellhounds, and a shit ton of money...Erica doesn't like their odds, but she hopes they're safe, that they've managed to get away. Hell, they could be heading to the same cave as her.

After a few hours, they pass the state line and Erica's stomach turns. She tells herself she's doing the right thing, and after a few more miles, she believes it. The nerves in her stomach turn into something else. Sparks of excitement. Finally, she is on the right path. She is doing something good. Perhaps what she was born to do. And it's got nothing to do with Sarah. Her old friend may have started her on this journey, but it now belongs to Erica. Every choice from here on out.

She changes busses three times, and after three exhausting nights of stops in the middle of nowhere and the army storming the vehicle each time to check for passes, finally arrives on the outskirts of the forest. After walking the short distance from the bus stop and leaving the path for rougher terrain, the woods in the distance, the first doubts crawl into her consciousness. It's so dark. Darker than the rolling farmland of her Kansas home. Dark enough to hide any manner of insidious beings.

Erica removes her bow and quiver from her duffel and slings them over her shoulder for easy access. She's never had to use the weapon to defend herself, but she's confident she can take down anything nasty that crosses her path.

A piercing howl shatters the night. The forest is a mass of shadows, the moon a thin, cold slice against the sky. She rubs her eyes, her hands rough like sandpaper, and stretches her wings. Three days of this. She estimates three days until she reaches the cave. Flicking a leaf from her hair, Erica surveys the darkness, peering into the shifting shadows, trying to decipher a shape. After a few minutes, her eyes adjust and she takes her first few tentative steps into the woods.

The trail winds through a dense thicket, the kind that snags clothes and hides hungry creatures. Erica steels herself and moves forward, each step a herculean effort. She remembers what her mom said: "We comply. We do what our president says and we'll be safe. There's no need to make waves when we are all now adjusted. We're safe." *Safe*. The word rattles in her mind like a loose screw. What do her parents know about safety anymore?

Sarah wasn't safe when she took that nanite. How many more will die that way?

A sudden rustle to her left freezes her in place. Her heart hammers in her chest, a runaway drum. She crouches low, her wings curling around her like a technicolor shield. Two figures burst from the underbrush, locked in a violent dance. Adjusteds. One has the elongated limbs of a spider, the other a face more canine than human. They snarl and lunge, a blur of enhanced rage. Erica holds her breath, willing herself invisible.

The spider-limbed adjusted lands a killing blow, and the canine crumples, a lifeless ragdoll. Blood gleams like spilled rubies in the moonlight. The victor surveys the scene, chest heaving, then turns its midnight eyes on her.

Erica swallows, holds her breath as she reaches for an arrow from the quiver strapped to her back. Exhaling slowly, she nocks the arrow as the spider adjusted scuttles toward her. It raises four of its terrifying limbs, opens a mouth lined with vicious, blood-stained teeth, and screams.

She flinches, and the arrow goes wide, pinning one it the

adjusted's legs to a tree. But it's enough to hold it for a few seconds. With her hands trembling, she nocks another arrow. Aims. Exhales. Releases. Just as the adjusted tears its way free of the trunk, leaving a severed limb behind. This arrow flies true. Straight though one it the adjusted's revolting eyes. It shrieks, then crumples, falling in a heap at the base of the tree.

Erica shudders, bile surging up her throat, and retches in the bushes. She's never killed anyone before. Obviously. She's never even physically hurt anyone. But this spider thing isn't a person anymore. And it was him, or her.

When she's done throwing up, Erica moves away from the dead adjusted, wanting to get as far away from the scene of the crime as possible. The scent of iron and ozone lingers in the air, reminding her of the violence she didn't know she was capable of committing. She spends the rest of the night with her bow held in front of her and an arrow nocked, trying to control her shallow breathing.

She thinks about the unadjusteds, the many who will be making their way through these woods and must face monstrous adjusteds like the spider guy. Most of them won't have defensive skills. People will die. People are already dying. Like the unadjusteds she saw yesterday while waiting for one of her transfers, lined up like cattle on the side of the road. A woman with a baby, a tall boy with freckles, an elderly man clutching a walker. All of them unadjusted, unchanged, unprepared. A bulk patrol leader shouted commands, and the line shuffled into waiting trucks. The man's voice was grating, but not unkind. Almost apologetic. *This is for your own good*, he said. *For your survival.* But where were they being taken? What were they going to do with them? The memory leaves a sour taste in Erica's mouth.

Her wings droop with exhaustion, the colors leeching out like dye in a rainstorm. She needs to rest, but she's too scared, so she keeps walking. Once, the idea of living in a cave would have seemed absurd, something out of a shitty post-apocalyptic novel. Now, it's the only thing that makes sense.

Her foot catches on a root, and she sprawls forward, hands scraping on rocky earth. She lies there, letting the cool ground seep into her bones. *Just a minute*, she tells herself. Just long enough to gather what's left of her strength. She rolls onto her back and stares at the sliver of sky poking through the canopy. Stars wink at her, disinterested and cold.

With a groan, she pulls herself to her feet and takes inventory. Her clothes are a disaster: torn leggings, a once-green jacket now more hole than fabric. She looks like an extra from a zombie fashion show. Her wings, at least, are intact. She unfurls them, stretches the delicate structures, and gives a tentative flap. They shimmer with a weak, tired glow.

She keeps walking through the next day, and when night falls for a second time, her eyelids drooping, her limbs protesting, she curls into a hollow in the trunk of a tree. With one hand wrapped around her bow and the other around an arrow, she falls asleep, deeply and dreamlessly.

Halfway through the next day, when she's finished relieving herself in the bushes, she pulls up her trousers and turns to rejoin the path, but a hand grabs her shoulder, yanking her back. Erica's wings flare, a burst of startled color, and she spins around, nocking an arrow.

"Whoa, easy!" The tall figure takes a step back, hands held high in surrender. "It's me!"

"Addison?" Erica's eyes widen, then narrow. She lowers her bow. "What are you doing here?"

Addison shrugs, her willowy frame looming larger in the gloomy forest. "Same as you, I suppose. Trying to survive."

Relief washes over Erica, mingled with a tinge of guilt, and she lowers her bow. She'd forgotten about Addison, about all the unadjusted friends she used to have. Before the wings, before the popularity. Before everything.

"Are you alone?" she asks, peering past Addison's shoulder.

"For now." Addison's blue eyes flicker with an emotion Erica can't place. "My family is... managing. Are you going to the cave?"

Erica nods. "I thought I was the only one from back home."

"There are hideouts all over the country," Addison says. "But this is HQ. This is where the leaders are heading."

"How do you know that?" Erica asks.

"I'm unadjusted," Addison replies shortly. "I made it my business to know."

Erica nods, berating herself for her shallow thinking. Unadjusteds are fleeing all over the country, when they're not being rounded up into the backs of trucks. Drones in the sky. Army on the streets. Tracking dogs in the woods. Erica doesn't have her pass anymore, she left her phone on the bus. But her wings are a clear sign of which group she belongs to. Addison could pass for an adjusted too, with her extraordinary height.

"We can carry on together," Addison says.

It's then Erica notices the throwing stars slotted into Addison's belt. She and Sarah had been friends, bonded by mutual hobbies involving weapons.

Addison's eyes fall to the bow in Erica's hand. "Is that Sarah's?"

It hurts to hear the name spoken aloud, and Erica nods once more. "I learned how to shoot."

"I heard."

"For Sarah," Erica says softly.

"I get that. She'd be proud of you."

Erica struggles to get the next breath into her tightening lungs. "Thank you."

They walk along the path together. Erica removes an apple from her pack and chucks it at Addison, who gives her an appreciative nod and bites into the bruised fruit.

"I thought you'd be in Canada by now," Erica says between bites, remembering some gossip she overheard during a shift at the diner. "Weren't your parents planning to flee?"

Addison looks away, her long red hair a wavy curtain. "We tried. The border's tighter than we expected. We got separated." She turns back to Erica, her tall frame hunching.

"I'm so sorry."

Addison shrugs. "We'll figure it out."

What else is there to say? To do? Erica's parents are back home in Kansas, safe, going about their small lives. While Addison's large family is on the run.

"I kind of thought you'd take the Nanite Enforcement

Program in stride," Addison says. "Considering you're already an alt."

"Is that what you call us?"

Addison cocks a defensive shoulder. "Altereds. Alts. Whatever. I guess it doesn't matter anymore."

"I guess not."

Erica gives Addison at once over. The unadjusted girl has always been tall and striking, her family a clan of red-haired giants. In a world obsessed with modifications, they stood out as peculiar, almost freakish. Yet there is a certain pride in their unadjusted nature, a defiance that Erica admires. "I'm sorry," Erica says." A name doesn't mean shit. "This situation is much harder for you."

Addison kicks at the pinecones on the path as they walk. "We all make our choices."

"Like Dr. Melody and his daughter."

"The guy who invented nanites? What's up with them?" Addison asks.

"Apparently, they're on the run. His daughter, Silver, refused to take a nanite. So they took off. President Bear has offered reward money. A million each."

Addison raises both brows. "Jesus. That's a hell of a lot of cash. The call center will be getting a shit ton of fake sightings, I'm sure."

"Maybe real ones too," Erica says sadly.

They don't sleep, but walk continuously through the woods without a break, catching up on old times. She forgot how much she likes Addison. Because she ditched her when she grew her wings. Maybe she can make it right now.

When they reach the cave, they are filthy, exhausted, and starving.

Erica uncovers the branches hiding the entrance to the underground cavern and is surprised to find lanterns lighting a descending path inside. With a deep breath, in which she inhales nothing but damp limestone, she follows the hopeful lights.

Addison sticks close to her side, keeping her head low to avoid the uneven ceiling, a throwing star in one hand.

With Erica's wings folded and an arrow nocked, they emerge into an enormous cavern, the space more sensed than seen as the lantern light only goes so far at dispelling the darkness. But there are people gathered in the middle. A bulk she vaguely recognizes as a pro ballplayer, a girl around her own age with beautiful green bird wings, an older man with a limp, another teenager who is giving orders from a clipboard and has a pencil stuck behind his ear. A young girl wheels out of a passageway in a wheelchair and in the distance a dog barks.

"I think this it is," Addison says.

The teenager with the clipboard looks up, passes it off to someone else, and approaches them. "Welcome." He sticks out a hand, eyeing Erica's bow with interest. "I'm Matt, and you've just joined the resistance."

Erica lowers her bow and takes the offered hand, smiles for the first time in weeks. It makes her cheeks ache. But in a good way.

She can do good here. She can honor Sarah's memories and she can lay her demons to rest.

✖✖✖✖✖

Thank you so much for making it all the way to the end. I hope you have enjoyed Erica's origin story and are excited to discover the rest of the series. If you did, leaving a review is the best possible present for an author! You can do it here:

https://geni.us/EricaSwiftfield

✖✖✖✖✖✖

If you want to know what happens to Erica once she meets up with Silver and team, don't forget to check out *The Unadjusteds*:

https://geni.us/Theunadjusteds

✖✖✖✖✖

Or turn the page for a sneak peak of the next origin story, *Paige Starling*

Turn the page for a sneak peak of the next origin story, Paige Starling

FREEBIE

If you'd like to read the next book in the series for FREE, please sign up to my newsletter at

https://www.marisanoelle.com/subscribe/

And don't forget there are 10 more companion novellas in the series:

Silver Melody
Matt Lawson
Joe Rucker
Paige Starling
Hal Small
Kyle Lewis
Jacob Shea
Sawyer Watson
Addison Shields
President Bear

Turn the page for a sneak peak of the next origin story, Paige Starling

PAIGE STARLING

An Unadjusteds Story

MARISA NOELLE

The nanites saved her father…then they turned him into a monster.

When Paige Starling's father is diagnosed with terminal cancer, she'll do anything to save him—even if it means draining her college fund for an experimental nanite treatment. The microscopic treatment rebuilds him from the inside out, erasing the disease that was killing him. But the cure is only the beginning.

At first, the changes seem harmless—whiter teeth, a faster metabolism, a stronger body. But then the modifications escalate. Stronger. Faster. Better. That's what they promise. Paige watches as the man she loves disappears, replaced by someone who is never satisfied, always chasing the next enhancement. And he's not the only one.

Now, genetic alterations are becoming mandatory, and those who resist—like Paige—are running out of time. When her best friend, Carson, is taken for a "correction" nanite designed to rewrite who he is, Paige realizes resistance is no longer a choice.

As the world transforms around her, will she fight for her right to stay human…or lose herself to the future?

Read on for first chapter…

PAIGE STARLING
CHAPTER 1

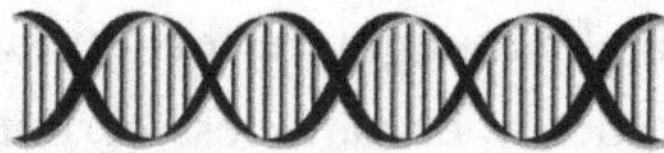

PAIGE HAS BEEN COUNTING the minutes—four hundred and seventy-three of them—since her father went through the door for the nanite treatment. Each second that passes brings him either closer to being cured or closer to...She won't let herself finish the thought. Instead, she stretches her legs across the sterile hospital waiting room and fixes her gaze on the swinging doors, willing them to open—with her father standing healthy on the other side.

"Want another cookie?" Her mother nudges the vending machine package toward her, smiling with effort that doesn't quite reach her eyes. The worry lines around her mouth have deepened over the past ten months, etching themselves into her once-flawless skin.

Paige shakes her head. The knot in her stomach has grown too tight for food. The nanite treatment—experimental, expensive, their last hope—plays on repeat in her mind. A single pill could rewrite her father's DNA, target the cancer cells, and eradicate them without the brutal side effects of the traditional treatments he's already endured. It sounds like magic, like science fiction, not something that could actually work.

Her mother's phone buzzes. "The bank confirmed the transfer went through," she whispers.

Paige nods. What's four years of university compared to a lifetime with her father? The math is simple, even for a fourteen-year-old. Still, the thought flutters through her mind that her future has suddenly become less certain, traded for her father's. She pushes it away. Selfish thoughts aren't welcome today.

The diagnosis struck ten months ago, thundering into their lives like a wrecking ball. Stage four pancreatic cancer. The words still make Paige's chest tighten, squeezing the air from her lungs as effectively as they did the first time the doctor spoke them.

She remembers her father sitting at the kitchen table that evening, his shoulders slumped in a way she'd never seen before. He'd always been larger than life—coaching her soccer team, spinning her mother around the kitchen to invisible music, hoisting Paige onto his shoulders even when she protested, "Too old for that, Dad." Cancer had shrunk him somehow, even before the weight loss and the treatments began.

"We'll fight it," he'd said, his voice cracking. "Every step of the way."

And they had. Chemo left him vomiting for days. Radiation burned his skin raw. Experimental immunotherapy gave him hives and fevers but did nothing to shrink the tumors. Until last week, when their oncologist had mentioned the nanites. The treatment had been around for a while, but it was expensive, and if it didn't cure you, it could kill you.

"It's not cheap," the doctor had warned.

Her father had laughed, a hollow sound. "What part of cancer is?"

Now, four hundred and seventy-eight minutes into waiting, the doors finally swing open. The doctor emerges first, and Paige's heart stops at the smile on his face. A real one, not the pitying grimace they've grown accustomed to.

"It took," he says simply.

And then her father walks through the door.

Paige's breath catches. He's standing straighter than he has in months, the yellowish tint to his skin already fading. His eyes—her eyes, emerald green and deep as forest pools—sparkle with something that looks suspiciously like hope. When he sees them, his face breaks into a grin that transforms him from the shell he'd become back into the dad she remembers.

"There's my girls," he says, arms outstretched.

Paige doesn't remember moving, but suddenly she's engulfed in his embrace, breathing in the hospital antiseptic and beneath it, the scent that is uniquely her father—cedar and coffee and home. Her mother joins the huddle, her slim arms encircling them both, and for the first time in ten months, they feel like a complete unit again.

"How do you feel?" her mother asks, voice trembling.

"Like I could run a marathon," he says, and there's wonder in his voice. "The pain...it's just gone. Like someone flipped a switch."

The drive home feels like a victory parade. Her father insists on stopping for ice cream. "Doctor's orders, gotta put on some weight."

They eat it in the car, laughing as it drips onto the leather seats her mother has always been so particular about. Paige savors the sweetness, the cold rush against her teeth, but mostly she relishes the sound of her father's laugh, unrestrained and full-bodied the way it used to be.

At home, they order in from all their favorite restaurants. Chinese and pizza and Thai, a feast to celebrate life reclaimed. Her father eats with gusto, something he hasn't done in months, and Paige feels something loosen in her chest.

"To nanites," her father toasts, raising his glass of beer. "The miracle of modern science."

They clink glasses, and Paige sips, but there's a flicker of unease beneath her joy. She's heard things about nanites at school, whispered conversations about kids who used them for enhancements rather than medical necessities. She's seen the effects too. How they've changed, become obsessed with the next upgrade, the next improvement. How friendships splintered between the "adjusteds" and "unadjusteds." How Renee now has butterfly wings, and Josh has bulked up with armored skin, and Pippa can run faster than a bullet.

But those were cosmetic nanites, she reminds herself. This was different. This was survival.

"What does it feel like?" she asks. "The nanite?"

Her father considers, chopsticks paused midair. "Like...imagine having a million tiny workers inside you, all focused on fixing what's broken. You can almost feel them buzzing around, rebuilding." He smiles. "Like magic, but science."

Later that night, after her mother falls asleep on the couch, Paige sits with her father on the back porch, watching the stars come out one by one. Crickets chirp in the grass. The sound of a dog barking in a distant yard reaches her ears. A few shouts from local teens prowling the neighborhood interrupt the peaceful night.

"I'm sorry about your college fund," he says quietly. "We'll build it back up. I promise."

Paige shrugs. "It's okay. I'm just glad you're here."

"I'm not going anywhere now, kiddo." He wraps an arm around her shoulders, pulling her close. "This is our second chance. Everything goes back to normal now."

She leans into him, finally letting go of all the stress she's been carrying for the last six months.

"Mom said they're running tests later this week to confirm the cancer is gone?"

"Just a formality. I can feel it, Paige. Whatever those nanites are doing, it's working. I'm back." He squeezes her shoulder. "And I won't waste a minute of it."

When she finally goes to bed, Paige lies awake staring at the glow-in-the-dark stars her father helped her stick to her ceiling when she was eight. The constellations they created together—some real, some invented—shine down on her like promises.

She thinks about what it means to be whole again. About the college fund that will be replenished. About family dinners and soccer games and her father growing old enough to see her graduate, marry, have children of her own. All the futures that were fading from possibility now restored by a single pill, a microscopic army rebuilding what cancer tried to destroy.

Nanites. The word rolls around in her head, fascinating and slightly terrifying. One small thing that changed everything.

If you'd like to carry on reading, click here:
https://geni.us/PaigeStarling